Autumn made her way into the kitchen.

He gestured toward his kitchen table where two mugs were laid out next to a teakettle and a plate of gingersnaps and scones. Autumn sat down across from Judah and began adding sugar and milk to it.

"You still like it sweet, huh?" Judah asked, a smile twitching at his lips.

Autumn had always had a sweet tooth. Judah used to tease her about it all the time when they'd been involved. Between milk chocolate bars and brownies, Autumn had always been craving something sweet to nibble on. "What can I say?" she asked. "Old habits die hard."

For a few moments, they both focused on their tea without any conversation.

"It's a bit strange sitting across from one another after all this time," Autumn said, eager to fill up the silence.

Judah held his mug between his hands and locked eyes with her. "I suppose so, although I always imagined you coming back home. You fit here, Autumn. I'm not sure why you ever left."

Because of you, she wanted to say.

Belle Calhoune grew up in a small town in Massachusetts. Married to her college sweetheart, she is raising two lovely daughters in Connecticut. A dog lover, she has one mini poodle and a black Lab. Writing for the Love Inspired line is a dream come true. Working at home in her pajamas is one of the best perks of the job. Belle enjoys summers in Cape Cod, traveling and reading.

Visit the Author Profile page at LoveInspired.com.

Her Alaskan
Return

Belle Calhoune

LOVE INSPIRED
INSPIRATIONAL ROMANCE

LOVE INSPIRED®

INSPIRATIONAL ROMANCE

Recycling programs
for this product may
not exist in your area.

ISBN-13: 978-1-335-58563-9

Her Alaskan Return

Love Inspired
22 Adelaide St. West, 41st Floor
Toronto, Ontario M5H 4E3, Canada
www.LoveInspired.com

Printed in U.S.A.

Fear thou not; for I am with thee: be not dismayed;
for I am thy God: I will strengthen thee; yea,
I will help thee; yea, I will uphold thee with
the right hand of my righteousness.
—*Isaiah* 41:10

For my mother, Anne Bell.
For teaching me the important lessons
and being such a masterful storyteller.

Chapter One

A fierce Alaskan wind had kicked up over Kachemak Bay, causing large, choppy waves to churn ferociously. Judah Campbell breathed in the briny scent of the sea as he hauled in his catch of the day with a ring net. His crew celebrated with excited shouts and kudos as they spotted the bright-colored crustaceans. It was unusual for fishermen to find red Alaskan crab in February. The season for catching crab was getting shorter and shorter. Kachemak Bay was well-known for herring, salmon and halibut. This time of year certain fish were limited due to weather conditions. Finding the red Alaskan crabs made Judah feel triumphant. At this point in his life, joyful moments were rare. He intended to savor this victory.

Salmon. Halibut. He'd reeled in both over the course of the day as well as the precious crab and some clams. As an Alaskan commercial fisherman, this was his livelihood, one he deeply enjoyed. For generations, Campbells had made their living in this manner, going all the way back to his great-grandfather. Serenity Peak was only accessible by air and water, which heightened the importance of the local fishing industry. Being out on the water for so many hours allowed him to enjoy the great outdoors and to contemplate his life. Not that he had much of a life these days. Tragedy and loss had shattered him.

After his fishing boat docked back at the harbor, his crew busied themselves placing the fish on ice in boxes and making sure everything was set up for the next day. They were a well-oiled machine, having worked together for a number of years.

"Hey, guys, why don't you head out? I'll finish up," Judah called out after a few hours of solid work. He stayed behind to clean the boat and spray down the holds, knowing he didn't have anyone waiting on him at home. Gone were the days when his son would greet Judah at the door and the aroma of Mary's cooking would assault his senses the moment he stepped in the house. That knowledge caused a dull ache in the center of his chest. For all intents and purposes, he was alone.

Judah headed toward his truck in the marina parking lot and let out a sigh as he got behind the wheel and began the drive home. The rain was really coming down, and visibility was poor. He flicked on his windshield wipers and focused on the road ahead of him. Suddenly, he spotted a figure at the side of the road. Judah slowed down. A woman was standing in front of her hood being pelted by the pouring rain. He couldn't make out who it was, but it bugged him to see anyone on their own in this type of weather. Judah jerked his truck to the side of the road and parked a few feet away. As soon as he stepped down from his truck he made his way over to the vehicle, doing a double take in the process. This was one of his best friend Sean's trucks. He would know the apple red color anywhere. Had Sean loaned someone his truck?

"Hey! Is there anything I can do to help?" he asked, shouting to get the lady's attention above the sound of the torrential downpour.

The woman raised her head. Light brown eyes flecked with caramel stared back at him. Judah let out a gasp. His heart lurched clumsily in his chest. Never in a million years could he forget her eyes.

"Autumn?" he asked as shock roared through him. It had been almost eight years since he'd seen her and twelve since they'd been a couple, yet her stunning features were unmistakable. Even drenched in rain she looked wonderful. High cheekbones and warm brown skin set in a heart-shaped face tugged at him. She'd always packed quite a punch, and the years had done nothing to change that fact.

"Judah!" she said, sounding equally surprised.

"Are you all right?" He reached out and gently grasped her arm. Like the rest of her, it was soaking wet.

"Yes," she answered with a jerk of her head. "The truck wouldn't start so I figured looking under the hood might help me figure things out. This rain is ice cold." She began shivering, teeth chattering. "My cell phone died so I couldn't call a mechanic."

At the moment he was worried about Autumn freezing to death in the frigid Alaskan temps. She needed to be warmed up immediately.

"Come on and get in my truck," Judah said, gently grasping her arm and leading her toward his ride. Once she was inside he went around to the driver's side and hopped in. He quickly dialed a local mechanic with instructions on where to find Sean's truck.

"Autumn, you need to get out of these drenched clothes ASAP. Where are you staying?" he asked.

"I'm living with Cecily until I can find my own place," she said, folding her arms around her chest.

Autumn and her younger sister had never gotten along very well, so the living arrangement was interesting in Judah's opinion. Maybe the years had softened their relationship. He sure hoped so for both their sakes.

Judah shrugged out of his warm winter parka. "Put this on and ditch that coat," he instructed, handing it to her. "Why don't I bring you to my place so you can warm up? It's only five minutes down the road. It'll take you much longer to get to your sister's house," he suggested. By that time, she would be a Popsicle. Autumn slid her arms into his jacket while he placed her sopping wet coat in a plastic bag.

"Considering I'm drenched to the bone, I'll take you up on that," Autumn said, her voice trembling with cold.

Judah held out his hand as Autumn struggled to put her left arm in the coat. She still didn't look one hundred percent well, but once she warmed up a bit he suspected that would change. Being pelted with ice cold rain had no doubt been a shock to the system.

As she shifted her body, Judah's eyes went straight

to her rounded belly. There was no mistaking the fact that she was expecting a baby.

"You're pregnant?" he asked, the words flying out of his mouth before he could rein them back in. He couldn't hide the surprise laced in his voice. Autumn was his age, thirty-nine going on forty. If they had stayed together and gotten married, he and Autumn might have had their own child by now. His chest tightened as painful memories of their breakup crashed over him. He shook them off and stuffed them down into the dark black hole he reserved for all of the agonizing moments that had gutted him over the course of his life. It did no good to dwell on past hurts. All it ever did was make him feel depressed.

He couldn't afford to let himself backslide, not when he'd worked so hard to move past all of the moments that had threatened to break him.

Autumn saw the stunned expression on Judah's face. It wasn't the first time she'd been on the receiving end of such a perplexed look. Being almost forty and pregnant tended to raise eyebrows. With Judah, things were more complicated, due to their tangled past. Seeing her protruding belly no doubt brought him back in time to when his own wife had been pregnant with his son. Losing a child in a terrible car accident wasn't something a person ever truly got over, especially when having a family was all he'd ever wanted.

"Yes, Judah," Autumn acknowledged with a nod. "I'm pregnant."

Judah gently placed her arm into the coat and said,

"Let's head to my house. I'll blast the heat to get you warmed up. How does that sound?" In response, Autumn nodded her head. She rubbed her hands together as the heat slowly began to fill the space.

Judah Campbell was still a good-looking man with a rugged physique, a strong jawline and eyes as blue as an Alaskan sky. There was a slight growth of hair on his chin and above his mouth, as if he hadn't shaved in a few days. After all these years he was still achingly handsome. But there was an air of sadness that hung over him. This man was miles apart from the one she'd once loved.

Oh, Judah. It wasn't supposed to be like this. In setting him free twelve years ago, Autumn had believed she'd been paving the path for his happily ever after. Things hadn't quite worked out the way she'd imagined.

A few seconds later Judah was driving down the road away from the fishing pier.

"I apologize if I reek of fish. After so many hours on the boat it tends to cling to me," Judah explained.

Although Autumn had detected a strong fish odor, it was the least of her concerns at the moment. Getting warm was at the top of her agenda. At this point even her bones felt cold.

"No worries. I'm just grateful for your help," she said. "I'm not sure what I would've done if you hadn't driven by."

"Happy to be there." Judah turned toward her. "What were you doing at the pier?"

She wrinkled her nose. Going out on the pier in bad weather hadn't been her most brilliant move. "There was a sea lion in the water that I wanted to take a picture of so I walked out on to the pier. I should have turned back when I realized it was starting to storm. Long story short, when I headed back to Sean's truck it wouldn't start." She shivered. "Of all the times for my phone to die on me."

"You've got to make sure it's charged, Autumn. What if you have an emergency with the baby?" he asked.

She hated to admit it, but Judah was right. It had been irresponsible of her to place herself in this position. Feeling humbled, Autumn didn't have the heart to respond.

"I know from what Sean told me that you're a writer in New York City," Judah said. He was clearly trying to fill the silence with conversation.

She always forgot that her brother Sean and Judah were still such good friends. From what she'd heard, Judah didn't have much to do with most of the townsfolk in Serenity Peak. She didn't know the whole story, but it was tied up in the loss of his wife and son.

"Yes. I love being a writer. It's a gift to be able to do something you enjoy, much like yourself." Judah had always yearned to be a commercial fisherman, following in his father's footsteps. He'd always said that the ocean brought out the best in him. She prayed that was still true.

Autumn couldn't get over the shock of coming face-to-face with her first love in such dramatic circumstances. According to Sean, Judah had become a bit of a hermit over the past few years, so she truly hadn't expected to see him so soon. "I'm grateful you were nearby to help me. I don't want to think about how long

I might have been out there in the rain if you hadn't rescued me."

"I'm glad I was there too. That's the true beauty of a community, banding together to help one another. Or that's the way it should be." A tremor jumped along his jawline. His words sounded sarcastic to Autumn's ears. She had a feeling he was referencing something personal.

Judah began to navigate the truck onto the main road. Autumn drank in the sights of Serenity Peak that she hadn't seen in years. The craggy facade of the Serenity Mountains. A small seaplane as it dipped down across Kachemak Bay. A bald eagle soaring gracefully in the sky.

"I had no idea you were back in Serenity Peak. When did you come home?" Judah asked.

Her teeth began to chatter. She was still chilled to the bone. "J-just yesterday, Judah. I flew in from Fairbanks."

"Any reason you came back? I thought you were eager to get away from small towns and Alaska."

She cringed. Judah was bringing up one of their last face-to-face meetings. At the time, Autumn had been young and desperate to sever all ties with Judah and her small town. She'd said so many things she really hadn't meant to cover up her broken heart. Breaking up with him had been her misguided attempt to make sure Judah was able to live out his dream of having children. She had sacrificed her own happiness so he could become a father one day.

"That was a lifetime ago. So much has changed since then," she acknowledged.

"I won't argue with you on that point," Judah conceded, making a face.

"I'm already five months along with my pregnancy. I've given it a lot of thought and I want to raise my child here in Serenity Peak where I grew up. I'm thinking of this as a permanent move." Autumn's childhood had been wonderful. She and her three siblings had been well-loved by their parents. Alaska had been a great stomping ground for their adventures. She wanted no less for her little one. "I'll be able to work remotely while being employed as a writer."

Judah said, "Your plan makes sense. There's no better place to live than Alaska." A quick glance in his direction showed a shuttered expression. He seemed incredibly guarded, so much more so than when they'd been head over heels in love with one another. It hadn't escaped her notice that Judah hadn't congratulated her for being pregnant. What did she expect? He'd lost so very much in his own life. Why should he be happy for her?

"I was sorry to hear about your wife. And your son," Autumn said. She knew that she was dodging landmines in bringing up Judah's family tragedy, but she couldn't ignore it. Losing his wife, Mary, and their son so horrifically must have been devastating for Judah. Ever since then, according to Sean, Judah had been a loner, cutting himself off from the residents of Serenity Peak. All she knew from Sean was that someone had started a cruel rumor that Mary had been on pills before the crash. Autumn didn't know much more than that tidbit. It had been enough to alienate Judah from the townsfolk in Serenity Peak.

Judah clenched his jaw. "Thanks," he said tersely. "Life isn't always fair."

An awkward silence filled the air until Judah turned down a road lined by snow-covered Sitka trees. He pulled into a driveway leading to a modest, log cabin style home. Autumn knew immediately that this was a far cry from the home Judah had grown up in and had inherited from his dad. She wasn't surprised he had renovated the place to meet current trends. The Campbell family's house had been old-fashioned and in need of updates. Regardless of that detail, the home had always been full of love.

After putting his truck in Park, Judah quickly made his way to the passenger side and helped her down. He was still a gentleman, she realized. These same gestures had been one of the reasons she'd fallen so fast and hard for him. He had made her feel incredibly safe and well loved.

As they walked along the snowy path toward his house, Autumn spotted two cedar Adirondack chairs sitting on his front porch. She knew without asking that they were Abel Drummond's creations. Among other things, he was an accomplished woodworker. His craftsmanship had always been impeccable.

Judah opened up the door and ushered her inside from the cold. Although she'd warmed up in the truck, her wet clothes still felt uncomfortable. As it was, she didn't want to drip on his gleaming hardwood floors. She was beginning to feel like an imposition.

The sound of nails clicking on the hardwood floors heralded the arrival of a medium-sized Irish setter who flew to Judah's side. "Hey, Delilah," he said, bending over and lavishing the dog with attention. "Did you miss me, girl?" Delilah answered by licking the side of Judah's jaw.

"She's a beauty," Autumn said, admiring the glossy sheen of Delilah's coat. She hoped to get a dog of her own when her child was a bit older.

"She is. I have a dog walker who comes to the house a few times a day when I'm working so she's not cooped up. Delilah loves the outdoors."

The canine began curiously sniffing Autumn, who patted her on the head in return.

"Okay, that's enough girl," he said, gently pushing the Irish setter. He swung his gaze to Autumn. "Why don't you take a hot shower in the guest bedroom bathroom? While you're in there I'll put some clothes on the bed for you. I'm going to take one myself to wash my day at sea off. Then I can make us some hot tea. Sound good?"

"Yes, it does," she said, feeling comforted by the idea of a shower and some soothing tea. Autumn followed after Judah as he led her down the hall.

"Everything you need will be in the bathroom closet. I'll see you in a bit," Judah said with a nod.

Autumn went into the bathroom, shutting the door behind her. She peeled off her wet clothes and hopped into the shower. She shut her eyes as the warm water cascaded over her body. She took her time warming up before toweling off and heading into the bedroom. A stack of clothes awaited her—a hunter green sweatshirt, thick socks, a pair of sweats.

They were men's clothing so Autumn didn't have to

deal with the discomfort of wearing his deceased wife's apparel. Even though the items were big on her, Autumn felt wonderful being in dry clothes. When she made her way into the kitchen, Judah took her wet clothes and placed them in the dryer. He gestured toward his kitchen table where two mugs were laid out next to a tea kettle and a plate of ginger snaps and scones. Autumn sat down across from Judah and began adding sugar and milk to it.

"You still like it sweet, huh?" Judah asked, a smile twitching at his lips.

Autumn had always had a sweet tooth. Judah used to tease her about it all the time when they'd been involved. Between milk chocolate bars and brownies, Autumn had always been craving something sweet to nibble on. "What can I say?" she asked. "Old habits die hard."

For a few moments they both focused on their tea without any conversation.

"It's a bit strange sitting across from one another after all this time," Autumn said, eager to fill up the silence.

Judah held his mug between his hands and locked eyes with her. "I suppose so, although I always imagined you coming back home. You fit here, Autumn. I'm not sure why you ever left."

Because of you, she wanted to say. *And Mary.* A few months after her breakup with Judah he'd started dating Mary. Seeing them together had nearly ripped her heart out. She had almost run back to Judah and begged him to take her back. Leaving had been her only sensible option. How could she have stuck around and watched Judah fall in love with another woman? To marry Mary and build a family with her? It would have cut sharper than a knife. Being on the East Coast had allowed her to build a life without having to watch Judah live out his dreams with someone else. But she couldn't say any of those things because Judah had no idea of the huge secret she'd kept from him for all of these years. She would have given anything to carry his child and make a life with him.

Her doctor had informed her that due to severe endometriosis she would never be able to conceive a child. As she struggled to accept the devastating news, Autumn had decided to end things so Judah could move on and have the family of his dreams. Only she hadn't told him about her inability to bear future children. Knowing Judah, he would have sacrificed his wishes for a family to be with her. And she would never have forgiven herself. And he would have grown to resent her.

God worked in mysterious ways. Finally, so many years after her shocking diagnosis, Autumn was pregnant. She'd long since given up on hoping for a child of her very own, so this was truly a gift from above. Even though her marriage to Jay had ended in divorce due to his infidelity, she was grateful for this baby. A dream come to fruition.

Thank you for this blessing, Lord.

"Well, I'm home now," she said, pushing away the old memories, choosing instead to focus on the here and now. It was all in the past. With a baby on the way, Autumn's future was clear. She would make her child her number one priority. Part of doing so was ensuring that she still had a career in journalism. Being able to work remotely from Serenity Peak was an incredible blessing. If she had to travel from time to time to investigate leads, Autumn would make that work as well. Having family nearby would be crucial to her plans.

"You've completely renovated the place. I wouldn't even recognize it." Back in the day she'd sat at the Campbells' dinner table countless times and enjoyed Mama Campbell's down-home cooking. The home still had a rustic vibe, but she could no longer view it as old-fashioned. He'd brought it into the twenty-first century.

"Yeah," he acknowledged with a bob of his head. "It was Mary's idea. She thought it would breathe new life into the place."

Autumn didn't know what to say. It was terribly sad that Mary was no longer around to enjoy seeing her plans come to pass. "Well, she did a beautiful job. It's lovely." She picked up another scone and bit into it, enjoying the flavorful berry taste as it landed on her tongue.

"Is your husband arriving soon?" Judah pressed, his eyes brimming with curiosity.

She sucked in a fortifying breath before answering. "I'm not married anymore. The divorce papers were already in progress when I found out that I was expecting." She placed her hand on her belly, noticing how Judah's gaze landed on her abdomen before quickly glancing away.

"And you didn't want to try and save the marriage?" he asked, his eyes widening.

Autumn took a deep breath before responding. How many times had she been asked this question by well-meaning friends back in New York? Too many to count if memory served her correctly. Explaining was never easy.

"It was beyond salvaging. We had too many lifestyle differences to make it work." She sensed from the look etched on Judah's face that he wanted her to elaborate. "He's a musician who tours around the country a lot. And when he's not touring he does gigs that don't end until the wee hours of the morning. The two of us barely saw each other and then he had an affair with one of his backup singers that went on for months," she admitted. This was her truth and even though she feared being judged for the hard choices she'd made, Autumn wanted to be honest. It had taken her a long time to get past feeling ashamed that she hadn't lived out her happily ever after. She bit her lip. "We tried to make things work for a very long time, but all we did was argue. Neither one of us wanted to live that way."

"And the baby?" he asked, his voice sounding gruff. "It'll be tough being a father all the way from New York City, won't it?"

"The doors will always be open for him to be involved in his child's life. I would never take that away from him. On my end I'll do everything possible to make sure he can serve that role if he wants to," Autumn said. And she meant it. "To be honest, having this baby is a blessing. If I end up doing it all by myself, I'll embrace my role as mother with open arms."

She didn't want to get into it with Judah, but Autumn

wasn't sure her ex-husband saw a place in his life for a child. That was one of the most painful parts of her marriage. She'd been only in her early twenties when told she could never bear a child. She'd carried that pain around with her for a very long time. Her infertility had never mattered to Jay, but in hindsight, she now knew it had been his preference to be a permanently childless couple. His reaction to her pregnancy news had been a mixture of disappointment and anger. He'd expressed to her that he had never wanted a child and couldn't imagine his life as a father. That had spoken volumes. She'd known at that point that their lives were on different paths and that the decision to file for divorce had been the right one. Finding out about his affair had truly shattered their marriage.

God offered up blessings when you least expected it. This baby was an absolute gift from above. She would make motherhood her main priority. Autumn had no intention of squandering this chance.

Coming home to Alaska wasn't as simple as she'd conveyed to Judah. She hadn't told him everything, although she knew he would find out soon enough. Gossip flew around Serenity Peak like high-flying kites. Autumn now worked for the *Alaska Tribune*. She'd been hired to write about the local Alaskan community, starting with an article about the commercial fishing industry in the Kenai Peninsula. Her initial research had uncovered the possibility that there was a federal investigation being launched into acts of fraud being committed by commercial fisherman, allegations that could lead straight back to Judah.

Chapter Two

Once Autumn's clothes finished drying, Judah waited in the kitchen as she changed back into her attire. He was still trying to wrap his head around the events of the past few hours. Not only was Autumn back in Serenity Peak, but she was pregnant and he'd rescued her from a torrential downpour after her car broke down. Although they'd parted ways twelve years ago, the memories of their love story were still sharp in his mind. He and Autumn had been together for a period of seven years. They had started dating each other when they were twenty.

Judah had wanted her to be his girlfriend since they were teenagers, but out of respect for Sean, he'd steered clear of her. Autumn had been the one to pursue him when they grew older, and with Sean's approval, they had become a couple.

At one point in time Judah had believed they would grow old together. He had even made plans to restore his mother's engagement ring and propose to Autumn.

Judah had only waited to make sure Fishful Thinking got off the ground and he could make a comfortable living for them. He let out a brittle laugh. Those dreams had crashed and burned. To this day he wasn't all that certain why Autumn ended things between them, but for Judah it had been heart-wrenching.

A heads-up that Autumn had returned would have been nice. He stuffed down a burst of irritation that Sean hadn't told him she was coming home to Serenity Peak. He was his best friend—one of his only buddies in Serenity Peak. After the accident and the disgusting rumors about Mary, Judah had cut his ties with almost everyone in town. Every now and again Sean gave him little breadcrumbs about Autumn's life. A part of him had always felt disloyal to Mary for craving such tidbits about his ex-girlfriend. It wasn't that he'd carried a torch for her, but he had always been curious about her life away from Alaska.

Seeing her rounded belly had caused a groundswell of grief to rise up inside of him, not only for the dreams he'd once harbored for the two of them but for his son, Zane. Sometimes it all hit him at the most unexpected times—a feeling of loss as deep as the ocean. Even as a kid it had been Judah's desire to have a house full of children he could raise and shower with love. Those hopes had been snuffed out by events outside of his control. He'd held his tongue while talking to Autumn about her ex-husband. What kind of man, he wondered, wouldn't want to be a part of his child's life? It was unfathomable.

His cell phone rang, and he saw Brody Locke's name

pop up on his caller ID. Brody was a member of Judah's crew. He'd shown himself to be loyal and hardworking over the past five years. He was also someone Judah knew he could trust implicitly.

"Hey, boss," Brody said. "I wanted to discuss something with you if you have a few minutes."

"Hi, Brody. Is it all right if I circle back to you? It's not a good time for me to talk." A long pause ensued with no response from Brody.

"Is everything okay?" Judah asked after a few beats of silence.

Brody let out a ragged sigh. "I got some intel from a friend in Homer. A lot of wild rumors are circulating that you might want to hear."

Judah clenched his teeth. Gossip had been circulating for weeks about a federal investigation into reporting irregularities. Although he had tried to discount the rumors as nonsense, the chatter was getting too loud to ignore. It was hitting way too close to home. This wasn't the first time word had gotten back to him either. According to the rumor mill, Fishful Thinking seemed to be in the crosshairs, which made absolutely no sense. Judah would never fail to report his catch or doctor his logbooks. He was an ethical fisherman who couldn't live with himself if he broke the rules for profit. He knew some fishermen caught more fish than was legally allowed, deliberately mislabeled fish or ventured into areas that were off limits to secure certain fish, but he wasn't one of them. He made his living honestly.

"Let's grab some coffee outside of work," Judah suggested. "Thanks for looking out for me, Brody. I'll talk to you later." His chest swelled at the loyalty Brody exhibited.

The sound of light footsteps alerted him to Autumn's approach. As she walked over the threshold to the kitchen, Judah sucked in a steadying breath at the sight of her. The ensuing years had only served to heighten her beauty. Tall and lean, in another life Autumn could have been a model gracing the covers of magazines or an Olympic athlete. But those endeavors had never appealed to her. She had always been interested in writing and the arts.

"I feel almost back to normal. And no longer like a drowned rat," Autumn said, smiling. "Judah, I can't thank you enough for being so gracious."

"You don't have to thank me. I would have done it for anyone." He saw Autumn flinch in response to his comment. *Why had he spoken so roughly?* Perhaps it was tied up in their past relationship and the way things had ended between them. Losing Autumn had truly crushed Judah. She had abruptly broken things off with him and he wasn't even certain what had gone wrong. One day she'd been in love with him and in the next, she'd wanted to end things. Judah had always felt that Autumn had given up on their relationship while he'd fought to keep them together. He couldn't help but wonder if she was doing the same thing with her husband.

"I should get out of your way," Autumn said. "Would you mind dropping me off at my sister's now? Hopefully I'll get word tomorrow about Sean's truck."

"Sure thing," he said. "Let me grab our coats. Come on, Delilah. You can come for the ride." Delilah began wagging her tail before running over to the front door to wait for them.

Judah brought Autumn the long olive green parka and held it out for her to slip her arms through. In the process his fingers brushed across her arm, causing a frisson of awareness to wash over him. It was muscle memory, he figured. His heart had belonged to her for so many years. He wasn't in love with her anymore, but it had taken him such a long time to get Autumn out of his heart and mind. She had been his entire world. To this day little pieces of her were imprinted on his heart.

Her face was impassive, as if she had no clue how she still affected him. *Good*, he thought. Judah didn't want Autumn to have that power over him. The way she had in their relationship when he would have grabbed the stars from the sky if she'd asked him.

Why was he dredging up the past? Doing so made him feel disloyal to his deceased wife. Mary had once accused him of using her as a rebound romance to get over Autumn. A part of him knew it was true, yet he'd never admitted it. He'd loved his wife, but what they'd shared hadn't been moonlight and roses. A flicker of memory flashed into his mind—Autumn with the wind blowing through her hair as she stood on the deck of Fishful Thinking as he navigated the boat across the bay. The rich sound of her laughter had made his soul soar.

Stop! That was a lifetime ago. He forced himself back to the present. Judah needed to get as far away as possible from Autumn. He couldn't drop her off at her sister's house fast enough. Moving forward was his main objective in life.

Getting caught up in his past with Autumn wasn't a good idea. Judah didn't think he would survive it a second time around.

Once again, Judah came forward to help her step up into his truck. Autumn had to admit she'd missed being in the presence of a gentleman who opened doors and held out her chair. At his core, Judah was a caretaker, Autumn realized. He'd always been invested in the welfare of others. She imagined he'd been that way with his family.

Some instinct told her that Judah didn't have guests often, which made his gesture to invite her over even more meaningful. Strangely enough, Autumn hadn't spotted a single photograph of Mary and their son. Not one. Matter of fact, Autumn hadn't seen any pictures at all on display. It was a bit odd considering how much family had always meant to him. Growing up in this very same house there had always been photos on every mantle and wall.

Perhaps he didn't want to be reminded of everything he'd lost. She felt a pang in her heart. She hated the fact that he'd endured so much. For a man like Judah who'd only ever wanted a family of his own, his current situation was devastating.

"The town feels different," Autumn noted as they drove past the town square and Fifth Street where most of the stores were located. She spotted several new shops—a charming bookstore–coffee shop, a lovely jewelry shop, as well as an artist's studio. Serenity Peak had always been a haven for creative people, so it was only fitting to see these specialty stores in existence.

"When was the last time you were here?" Judah asked. "Serenity Peak isn't the same place we grew up in."

"About three years ago. I came home for Skye's wedding." She let out a sigh. "Or should I say the wedding that wasn't. It was sad to see all of her hopes and dreams crushed." Perhaps she related to the young woman due to her own disappointments in her twenties. Heartache wasn't easy to live through. Frankly, she wasn't sure how she'd survived it.

Skye Drummond was the daughter of one of the founding families of Serenity Peak. They ran Sugar Works, a birch syrup company that sold all over the world. She was young and a bit on the wild side. Growing up, her older sister, Violet, had been Autumn's best friend. It wasn't any of her business, but Tyler Flint had been right to pull the plug on their wedding. Skye hadn't been ready to settle down. Not by a long shot. However, ditching someone so close to the wedding day was cruel. Autumn hated how Skye had been treated.

He nodded. "You're right," he acknowledged. "A lot has changed. We've had an influx of folks wanting to relocate here due to our healthy fishing industry and the hot springs. Not to mention Sugar Works is still a household name in Alaska. A lot of jobs have opened up there."

"Serenity Peak has always been popular with tourists looking for a tranquil Alaskan experience," she said. "No better town in the state to offer calm and serenity."

"I wouldn't describe this town that way, but then again, I'm an outsider these days. From time to time I run excursions on my boat for tourists, but other than that I keep away from the goings-on in town." Judah sounded so matter of fact, as if he couldn't care less about their hometown or the residents. His indifference was unsettling. It was as if he had retreated so far inside himself that the Judah she'd once known had disappeared.

"That's hard to picture." Although she knew that Judah harbored anger toward town residents, it was still hard to wrap her head around it. At the time of Judah's loss Autumn hadn't wanted to know all of the details about the town gossip. Being told by Sean that Judah was out of sorts and grieving had been painful to hear. Letting go of him all those years ago had been so he could live his best life. She'd never imagined he would lose so much. His world had collapsed in an instant. A tight feeling spread across her chest just thinking about it.

"Your family was always a big part of Serenity Peak. Town mayors. Shop owners. Teachers. The commercial fishing community. Has that changed as well?" she asked, filled with curiosity about the current state of affairs.

Judah shrugged. "I can only speak for myself. The fishing community is my only connection to this town. My nephew Ryan is now a member of law enforcement so I suppose the Campbells are still in the thick of things. He's grown up to be a good man."

Autumn could hear the pride ringing out in Judah's

voice. Ryan had been a child the last time she'd seen him, serving as a reminder of how many years stood between her and this town. She probably wouldn't even recognize him if she passed him on the street. Autumn didn't dare ask about Judah's brother, Leif. She knew they were estranged, but she didn't know the particulars. Yet another tremendous loss for Judah. He and Leif had always been joined at the hip.

"At least the economy is healthy. I've been hearing lots of stories about Alaskan towns that are struggling with their ability to keep their shops open and haul in plentiful amounts of fish. It's rough out there."

"My operation has been blessed, but the Alaskan fishing industry as a whole has been hit with fish shortages, which ultimately affects the bottom line." He cast a quick glance in her direction. "You seem pretty knowledgeable about Alaskan commercial fishing. Since when does it interest you?" he asked, his brows furrowed.

"Sean must've mentioned it in our conversations," Autumn answered. "He's got a vested interest in making sure the local fish supply is solid."

Her brother owned one of the most popular restaurants in Serenity Peak called Northern Lights. Seafood dishes were some of the establishment's most popular fare. Both of her parents worked there along with Cecily and other members of her large family. Judah had a share in the business but wasn't there often according to Sean. His main role was arranging for fresh fish deliveries several times a week.

Autumn felt a bit guilty. All of this information she'd

spouted about the commercial fishing business was material she'd researched in order to write her article. Was it wrong to withhold this information from Judah? It was awkward since his fishing operation was potentially under scrutiny. She'd always been professional as a journalist. Maintaining her standards in difficult circumstances was something she was proud of. Bending the rules wasn't her style. Not even for Judah and what they'd once meant to each other.

As they drove down the heavily forested mountain road, Autumn took a moment to soak in her surroundings. Wide-open spaces. Gorgeous trees blanketed in snow. A moose crossing sign—not exactly something you saw in New York City. This is what she had missed most about Serenity Peak. It offered a tranquility she'd never quite been able to find anywhere else. Judah put the brakes on as a graceful deer darted into the road. He glanced over at her. "Once you see one—"

"There's bound to be more," Autumn said, finishing his sentence. It was a Serenity Peak saying, one she'd heard hundreds of times ever since she was a child. Seconds later three more deer, including a foal, ambled across the road. Autumn let out a chuckle. The sight of the deer family made her feel all warm and fuzzy inside. She'd missed out on moments like this one. Never again would she take them for granted.

As soon as Judah pulled up in front of Cecily's modest ranch-style home, the front door flew open as if her sister had been expecting them. Within moments, Cecily came rushing toward the truck.

She seemed to catch Judah off guard by giving him

a bear hug as soon as he stepped out of the truck. All Autumn could do was watch as Judah squirmed. Her ex wasn't the most demonstrative person so she sensed his slight discomfort. Thankfully, Judah and Cecily were old friends. From the very first time Sean had brought him home the entire Hines family had fallen in love with him.

"Hey, Judah," Cecily said. "It's been ages since I've seen you. How are you doing?"

"Hi, Cici," Judah said, greeting her by her childhood nickname. "I can't complain. I've been keeping busy out on the bay. Even caught some red crabs. Still your favorite?"

"I could eat crab every day of the week," her sister replied. Her natural rapport with Judah made Autumn wish she could relax around him as Cecily did.

"Well, I'm going to get going. Gotta head out early tomorrow morning," Judah explained.

"Don't be a stranger, Judah," Cecily said, placing her hand on Judah's arm. "I've been making that mixed berry pie you used to love so much for the customers at Northern Lights. Just say the word and I'll save you some slices." With a wave, Cecily walked back toward the house.

Autumn envied their congenial relationship. Things felt so strained between her and Judah. Before they'd ever fallen in love, she and Judah had been the best of friends.

"Thanks again for the save, Judah," Autumn said. "I have no idea what would have happened if you weren't there." She owed Judah big-time.

"I'm glad I was at the pier at that exact moment in time," he said with a slight smile. For the first time since she'd seen him at the wharf he resembled the old Judah, the one who'd been full of light and laughter. With a nod he stepped up into his vehicle and got behind the wheel before roaring off.

After Autumn stepped inside the house she walked straight toward the kitchen in search of Cecily.

"What were you doing with Judah?" Cecily asked, wiggling her eyebrows as she turned toward her. Her sister had a huge smirk on her face.

Autumn counted to ten in her head. Suddenly it felt like they were back in high school all over again with Cecily being all in her business. Maybe she should have stayed with Sean and his family, but she had declined her brother's invitation. Having her as a houseguest would have overcrowded his modest sized home. As a result, she now had to deal with her sister.

"I'm not sure why it matters, but Sean's truck broke down and I was looking under the hood in the downpour. Judah drove by and spotted me right when I needed help." Just saying the words out loud sounded surreal. Cecily didn't need to know he'd taken her back to his place. If she did tell her sister the whole story, the news would be spread all around Serenity Peak in the blink of an eye. The entire town would be whispering about her and Judah reuniting at the harbor.

Her sister let out a tutting sound. "It didn't take you guys long."

Autumn folded her arms across her chest. "What is that supposed to mean?"

Cecily shrugged. "I knew you and Judah would be drawn to one another like magnets."

"It wasn't anything like that," she said with a shake of her head. "You know Judah. It would be impossible for him to keep driving once he spotted someone in need. I'm five months pregnant, and I haven't laid eyes on Judah in years. I can't believe you think I'm chasing after him."

"I wasn't suggesting anything of the sort!" Cecily huffed, placing her hands on her hips. "It's called chemistry. You and Judah have always had it. I was simply saying that I wasn't surprised to see the two of you together. Honestly, I never understood why the two of you broke up in the first place."

Autumn twisted her mouth. "That's old news. Sometimes things just don't work out. I don't understand why you're dredging up the past when we both moved on ages ago."

Her sister quirked her mouth. "I've always had the feeling that there was more to the story, but we've never been close as sisters, so I understand why you didn't confide in me. But I couldn't help but notice that after Judah started seeing Mary you moved away from Serenity Peak and created a new life for yourself. With a husband I might add. And now you're having the baby of your dreams as a single woman. You haven't lived here for over a decade. Why did you come back to Serenity Peak?"

The question gave Autumn pause. Why had she come back home after all this time? From the moment her doctor had confirmed Autumn's pregnancy she'd known that Serenity Peak would be her baby's home. There was no other place in the world Autumn would consider. Cecily was making her question her actions. Hadn't this been the right decision? Wasn't she wanted in her hometown? Now, with a few probing questions from Cecily, she was full of indecision.

Why did it rattle her so much to have come face-to-face with Judah? She'd fallen out of love with him a long time ago, but she couldn't pretend as if they didn't share a connection. She'd known him all her life. Seeing him again truly felt like a homecoming. If she had trusted him more back then, maybe she would have told him the truth about her infertility diagnosis. At the time she had been ashamed and worried that he might stop loving her. Sometimes it nagged at her. What might have been if she'd simply been honest. She had single-handedly destroyed their relationship.

Instead of answering Cecily, Autumn headed to the spare guest room to escape her sister's needling and lie down. Why had she accepted Cecily's offer to stay at her house? They had been at odds for most of their lives so she shouldn't be surprised that they were butting heads. Autumn placed a hand on her stomach and lightly rubbed it. She didn't need any additional stress in her life. At five months along, she was firmly established in her pregnancy, yet she also knew her age made this pregnancy high risk.

Please, Lord. Protect this precious life. Let me bring this child safely into the world with no complications.

Being back in Serenity Peak was going to be tricky with her pregnancy, finding a place of her own to live and investigating the piece she was researching on the local fishing industry. She would need to go out into the field to interview people in order to flesh out her article and talk to the authorities. Maybe even make some day trips to Homer and Fairbanks. She'd been hired by the *Tribune* as a full-time staffer and there were several other pieces she'd received the green light to write.

Autumn prayed nothing would lead back to Judah or his company despite the rumors swirling around about his operation. So far all it amounted to was speculation and gossip. In a small town like Serenity Peak, folks loved to run their mouths.

Judah had lost enough in his life over the years. Autumn didn't want to be the reason his life was turned upside down all over again.

Chapter Three

Bright and early the next morning, Autumn headed over to the doctor's office for a prenatal checkup. Despite reassurances from her doctor in New York, she continued to worry about something going wrong with her pregnancy. Thankfully, this appointment had been set up for her weeks ago to allay her fears. It was difficult to feel secure in carrying a baby at this point in her life. Autumn knew she would only be able to fully relax once her baby was safely delivered and given a clean bill of health. She was counting the days until she could hold the baby in her arms.

Dr. Poppy Matthews was a striking young woman with stunning African braids, a lovely mahogany complexion and a warm personality. She immediately put Autumn at ease by asking her to call her Poppy rather than the more formal Dr. Matthews.

"Thanks for having your doctor send your file to me, Autumn," Poppy said. "I was able to look through it so I have some background on your medical history."

Over the next half hour Poppy examined Autumn, went over her blood work and talked to her about upcoming tests.

A high-risk pregnancy. Chromosomal tests. Gestational diabetes test. A geriatric pregnancy. That one had caused her jaw to drop. She wasn't ancient by any stretch of the imagination, yet it seemed as if carrying a child at thirty-nine came with a lot of caution. Autumn swallowed past her nervousness.

"So, how are you feeling? You seem a bit overwhelmed," Poppy noted.

Autumn let out a sigh. So far she hadn't been able to confide in anyone about her pregnancy fears. She'd tried to project an air of confidence. It was nice to be able to confide in her doctor. "There are so many things to consider. I can't help but worry that my age is going to complicate this pregnancy. It's a bit overwhelming."

"Don't worry, Autumn. You're in great health. Any pregnancy over thirty-five is classified this way. There's no reason to think you won't carry this baby to term."

"Even though I was once told I would never be able to conceive?" Autumn asked, blinking away tears. Her endometriosis had been weighing on her mind. Would it affect her pregnancy or delivery?

Poppy's eyes widened. "Well, thankfully that isn't the case. It seems clear that the diagnosis was based on your endometriosis, which you've treated with surgery. That allowed you to get pregnant, which I'm guessing was a dream come true."

Autumn nodded. The condition had plagued her ever since her early twenties. Pain had been a part of her daily life for years. "Surgery was suggested by my doctor due to all the agony I was in. We never really talked about it reversing infertility." Due to her husband's lack of interest in having children, Autumn hadn't considered trying to get pregnant.

Dr. Poppy pointed at Autumn's abdomen. "Well, it did," she said. "You're really blessed. Some women struggle to conceive after thirty-five."

She mustered a smile even as her gut twisted. Autumn was over the moon about carrying this baby, but her whole life had been altered by that devastating news all those years ago. Her decision to end things with Judah had been a direct result of her infertility diagnosis. She had lost the love of her life and mourned the fact that she would never be a mother.

"There's no better way to convince you that the baby is fine than to let you see your little one with your own eyes," Poppy said with a smile. She instructed Autumn to sit back and lift up her shirt. "This might feel a little bit cold, but it'll be worth it," she said as she placed gel on her stomach and moved the probe in a circular motion.

Suddenly, Autumn could hear the sounds of a heartbeat and a small shape appeared on the screen that resembled a precious baby. Autumn let out a little cry as Poppy pointed out the head and spine.

"So, from what I see, your baby is doing beautifully." Poppy peered closely at the monitor. "I'm not able to determine gender due to the baby moving around so much, but maybe next time."

A tear slid down her face. "It's okay, Poppy. This appointment has been so reassuring. As long as I know everything is going smoothly, I can wait to find out. It will be a nice surprise."

Poppy grinned. "That's what I'm here for, Autumn. To help you through the rest of your pregnancy," she said, reaching out and squeezing Autumn's hand. "I'd like to see you again in four weeks. If anything arises, don't hesitate to reach out."

"I will," Autumn promised. She would do whatever was required to bring a healthy child into the world. God had given her a chance at motherhood just when she had believed that door was firmly shut.

Autumn felt as if she was floating on air as she left the doctor's office with a photo of her baby in hand. She couldn't stop gazing at the black-and-white image. And even though she was still a little scared of the risks related to her pregnancy, a fragile hope was blossoming inside of her.

The day after Judah rescued Autumn by the pier, he didn't waste any time heading over to Northern Lights restaurant once he finished work. They'd ended the day early due to inclement weather. Judah wasn't ever going to take chances with the crew or his vessel. He'd been a commercial fisherman long enough to know the hazards of Alaskan waters. It was achingly beautiful, yet deadly at times.

Sean hadn't picked up his calls last night which was unusual for his friend. Some instinct told him Sean was feeling guilty about not warning him that Autumn had returned to Serenity Peak. His friendship with Sean spanned decades at this point. They had become instant friends in the sandbox in nursery school. They'd remained close even after Judah and Autumn's breakup. Sean had supported him like no other after the loss of Mary and Zane. He was more like a brother than Judah's own actual flesh and blood.

Judah stood outside the restaurant for a moment, admiring the gray façade with the white shutters. Northern Lights sat atop a cliff overlooking Kachemak Bay with the Serenity Mountains serving as a magnificent backdrop. The view always managed to take his breath away.

Although he tended to avoid the popular establishment, it was the only surefire way to track Sean down. Judah was a silent partner in the restaurant, having joined forces with Sean when he opened it fourteen years ago. Judah had stepped away to focus on the commercial fishing industry, which was a much better fit for him than dealing with the public. He knew he was at his best out on the water where he could seek out adventures and not have to deal with people. Thankfully, Sean had understood and they'd worked out a perfect arrangement, which included Judah providing fish for the restaurant and stepping in from time to time.

The moment he walked through the doors of Northern Lights, Judah breathed in the aroma of freshly grilled fish and roasted vegetables as well as rosemary fries and steak. The variety of scents made his stomach grumble with appreciation. But entering the eatery felt like being center stage. Small Alaskan towns like Serenity Peak didn't allow for many strangers. A quick glance around confirmed the fact that all of the diners were town residents he'd known for most of his life. Judah nodded to several who greeted him as he made his way to the back rooms. There were others he looked straight past. He would never forgive them for the nasty gossip they'd spread about his wife after the car wreck.

"Hey, Judah! You're a sight for sore eyes." The gravelly voice washed over him like a cozy blanket. Wally Hines, Autumn and Sean's dad, had a distinguished appearance with a head full of gray hair, twinkling eyes and a pair of wire-rimmed glasses. The older man had always been a huge influence in Judah's life.

Judah leaned in for a tight hug. "Hi, Wally. Looking good there," he said as the embrace ended. "You've lost some weight, I see." Wally was always looking to lose some pounds around his midsection, and it appeared he'd succeeded.

"Ten pounds. Thanks for noticing. I've missed you, son," Wally said with a grin. "If you're looking for Sean he's in the back with his head buried in the books." He let out a warm chuckle. "He'll be happy to see you."

As soon as he pushed past the swinging doors, Judah spotted Sean Hines through his open office door. Sean was standing at his desk looking through a pile of paperwork. Sean had the physique of a linebacker. He'd played for a minor league football team before blowing out his knee and leaving those aspirations behind. Everyone in Serenity Peak loved Sean. Judah had always believed that the success of Northern Lights was tied up in Sean's popularity rather than the amazing cuisine.

He stood in the doorway with his arms folded across his chest. "Hey there, Sean. You're a hard man to reach."

His best friend swung his head up and grinned at him. "Judah. Sorry about not returning your calls. I've been up to my ears in delivery issues and illnesses amongst the staff. We've had to scramble to get replacements." Sean riffled through some papers on his desk then looked back at Judah. "What's up? I'm surprised to see you here."

"Don't start with that," Judah protested. "I work long hours out on the water. I promise I'm not avoiding you."

"It's not me I'm worried about," Sean said with a shake of his head. "It's the rest of the town."

Fair point. Judah didn't even bother to challenge Sean's comment. He had spoken nothing but the truth. Most people in town weren't a priority for him. Not after what they'd said.

"So why didn't you tell me that Autumn was coming home?" Judah asked. "I was pretty shocked to see her at the pier." Judah didn't mention that he'd taken her to his house to get warm. He would let Autumn disclose that detail to Sean if she so desired. It wasn't as if anything had happened, but it still felt like information he should keep quiet about.

Sean sank down into a chair. Light brown eyes locked with his own. "I told you a long time ago that I didn't want to get in the middle of anything between you and Autumn. I love you both too much to get involved."

Judah sat on the corner of the desk. "I'm not asking that of you. I just didn't like being caught off guard." Especially by his first love. Judah ran a hand over his face. He didn't have to add that Autumn had blindsided him once before by calling it quits on their relationship. Try as he might to stuff the memory down, it still stung.

"I get it, Judah. And I'm sorry. To be honest, it felt awkward telling you that Autumn was pregnant and coming home to raise her baby here," Sean explained, quirking his mouth. "Honestly, it was a surprise to all of us. A happy one though."

"Babies are always a blessing," Judah said. "I'll never forget the day Zane was born." At nine pounds seven ounces, Zane had come into the world during a brutal snowstorm.

Sean nodded. "Me neither. I was honored to be his godfather. I miss him too, Judah. More than you know."

Sean and Zane had been particularly close. His best friend had taught his son how to throw a football and how to make collard greens, pot roast and quiche Lorraine. Sean had been Zane's honorary uncle.

"I know you do," Judah said. "And if I've never told you, I'm grateful for your friendship. Things could have gotten awkward between us after Autumn and I broke up but you never wavered." It was hard for Judah to tap into his emotions, but Sean needed to hear this. It was way overdue.

"Are you kidding me? There's nothing that could ever break up the dynamic duo." Judah could see Sean was fighting back tears. He was a big old softie. "That would be like Batman without Robin."

"Ain't that the truth," Judah said with a grin.

Sean leaned across the table and leaned on his forearms. "How about we grab some lunch? We can sit at our old table."

Judah made a face. "Sounds good, but I don't want to—"

"Don't even say it," Sean said, slicing his hand through the air. "You keep telling me that you want to move forward, but you're still stuck. I know you carry a lot of anger in your heart, Judah, and I don't blame you. The rumors about Mary being on pills when she crashed the car were hideous. Vicious. But you can't take it out on the entire town. It's not healthy."

Judah held up his hands in defeat. "Okay. If it means you'll can the lecture, let's go eat." At this point he knew it was better to give in than to protest. Plus, he was trying to change. Eating lunch in the dining area wouldn't kill him.

Sean stood up and cuffed his hand around the back of Judah's neck. "Come on. Let's do this!" Within minutes they were seated at their old table with a magnificent view of the mountains and the sparkling waters of the bay.

"Hey, boys. What can I get for you?" The familiar honeyed voice caused him to swing his head up in surprise. Autumn, wearing a Northern Lights T-shirt, stood by their table, with a small pad in her hand. The smile etched on her face caused his stomach to painfully twist.

Judah looked over at Sean and raised an eyebrow. Yet another thing Sean hadn't thought to mention. Autumn was waitressing at Northern Lights! A sheepish expression crept on to his friend's face. Sean burrowed his head in a menu he knew by memory.

"You're working here?" Judah asked as his gaze turned back to Autumn.

"I'm just filling in as a favor to Sean," Autumn said, looking over at her brother. "Like old times."

"I thought you'd be writing," Judah said. He'd gotten the impression being a writer was her focus for employment in Serenity Peak.

"She's actually on assignment for the *Alaska Tribune* focusing on local stories," Sean chimed in. Pride rang out in his voice. "Autumn is their newest hire."

"Wow. That's big time," Judah said. "The *Tribune* is one of the largest news outlets in the state."

Autumn sent Sean a loaded look then shifted uncomfortably from one foot to the other. "Yes, it's a great job. I'm happy to work a few hours here and there, as long as it doesn't interfere with my main gig." She let out a chuckle. "It means big bro now owes me a huge favor."

Sean chuckled. "As long as it doesn't involve changing dirty diapers I'm okay with that."

Judah laughed along with them. The idea of Sean dealing with a dirty diaper wasn't something he could picture. Sean was married to a wonderful woman named Helene. They had three kids ranging in age from five to thirteen. As Sean often liked to say, he was done changing diapers. Been there, done that. Judah knew his friend was completely serious.

Autumn quickly took their order and promised to return with two waters. She'd seemed slightly on edge. Something was up with her. Judah knew her well enough to know when she was unsettled. The look she'd given Sean had hidden meaning. She'd been a nervous wreck with trembling hands. Judah couldn't help but wonder if it had something to do with the baby she was carrying. It was none of his business, especially since they had been out of each other's lives for more than a decade, but he prayed that she delivered a healthy baby. If not, Autumn would be shattered.

Autumn hated having a guilty conscience. Waiting on Judah and Sean was nerve-racking. Her brother had shaken her by mentioning her employment with the *Tribune* in front of Judah. What would she have said if Judah had asked her what stories she was working on? She wasn't prone to lying, but telling him the truth might prove to be awkward. Sean had previously told her that Judah was aware of fraud allegations being tied to the local fishing community. But did he have any idea that he and his operation might be under the microscope? Never in a million years could she imagine Judah underreporting his fishing hauls, mislabeling fish or catching fish in unauthorized areas. He was honest to a fault.

Judah was an honorable man. Or at least he had been back in the day. People didn't change who they were at their core.

Once Sean finished lunch with Judah and headed back to his office, Autumn followed behind her brother. She needed to warn him against telling Judah about her assignment from the *Tribune*. If necessary, Autumn would tell him herself.

Autumn entered Sean's office with purposeful strides. She felt like a kid who'd gotten their hand caught in the cookie jar. She'd only arrived in Serenity Peak a few days ago and she was already tiptoeing around.

"What's wrong?" Sean asked, knitting his brows together. "You look upset."

She twisted her mouth. "You shouldn't have mentioned my working for the *Tribune* in front of Judah," Autumn said. "I'm writing a piece on the local commercial fishing industry, Sean. Allegations of underreporting catch and falsifying records are serious. Judah's operation is one of the most profitable in this area. It stands to reason that he might be under scrutiny."

"So what? Are you saying that Judah is involved in something illegal?" Sean asked in a raised tone.

"I'm not saying anything of the sort." She let out a frustrated sound. "But it's my job to be as objective as I can in my reporting and follow where the story leads me." She didn't want to say even if it led straight to Judah.

A sound in the doorway caused Autumn to turn in that direction. Judah was standing there looking confused. "I came back to get my keys," he said, jerking his chin in the direction of Sean's desk where the keys sat. "Autumn. Please tell me you're not writing a hit piece about the local fishing industry."

"Judah. I can explain," she said, swallowing past the lump in her throat.

Sean threw up his hands and said, "This is between the two of you. Just keep it down to a dull roar." With a shake of his head, Sean left his office, closing the door behind him with a little bang.

Shivers ran down the back of her neck at the outraged

expression etched on Judah's face. She understood why Sean had bailed, but she wished he'd stuck around for moral support.

Judah scowled at her. "Can you really explain, Autumn? Because it appears that you're running around trying to dig up dirt on me and my business. This is serious stuff."

Shock roared through her at his accusation. "Surely you don't believe that. I would never do anything to cause you pain, Judah."

His eyes widened. "Are you kidding me? You have no idea of how much you once hurt me, and it appears that you're not finished twisting the knife." For a moment it seemed as if steam might come out of his ears. "Fishing is my life. My career. It's the only reason I get up in the morning." His voice rang out with outrage. "It's all I have in this world. If it's taken away from me, I really won't have anything left."

Chapter Four

Judah bolted out of Northern Lights without even waiting for a response from Autumn. So much emotion had risen to the surface in their encounter, he'd felt as if he was on the verge of an explosion. He knew that retreating from the situation was the only sensible option. He had so much built up inside of him that he was struggling to control. It had been this way ever since the accident, and although he was getting better at controlling his outbursts, he was still a work in progress. Judah didn't want Autumn to be on the receiving end of his anger. He would have a hard time living with himself if he continued to lash out at her. During the many years they had spent together, he could only remember one time when they had raised their voices at one another. Judah had stuffed down the memory of Autumn breaking up with him because it hurt too much to relive it.

His brown-eyed girl. That's what he had lovingly called her. Seeing her after all this time had dredged up a lot of memories.

He strode away from the establishment until he reached the fenced-in promontory where he could look out over the vast valley of Serenity Peak. The gleaming water sparkled below. Judah watched as a flock of birds dipped down to capture their fish of the day. The natural beauty of Alaska had a way of soothing his soul as nothing else ever could. Slow, deep breaths, he reminded himself.

Serenity Peak, Alaska, had once been his haven. In the last few years it hadn't served that purpose whatsoever. Not after the accident. If it wasn't for his home and the memories of his wife and son that would always be imprinted within those walls, he would've picked up and moved ages ago. His fishing career was all he had left, along with a few loyal friends like Sean and Brody.

"Judah." He let out a soft groan as Autumn's voice washed over him. She'd followed behind him without his knowing it. Judah didn't trust himself to turn around and face her. He was too emotional right now and Autumn was one of the few people who could make him feel vulnerable. He'd worked hard to develop his tough guy image.

Judah heard the crunch of footsteps in the snow, right before he felt her slight touch on his arm. He wanted to jerk away from her nearness, to run as far away as possible from her warm, brown eyes and the tender timbre of her voice.

"Judah. You completely misunderstood my conversation with Sean."

He whirled around to face her. "So you're not working

for the *Tribune* on a story about the commercial fishing industry? Did I get that wrong?"

"No, you didn't. I am," she admitted. "But I'm in no way focusing on you and Fishful Thinking as part of my article. As you know, there have been allegations floating around the area about reporting irregularities and fraud. My assignment is to write about the local fishing industry and report on it for the *Tribune*. My focus is on all the fishermen from this area, not just you."

A little of his defensiveness fizzled out. "I just hope my operation doesn't get dragged under. My professional reputation is at stake." He wanted to make it clear to Autumn that he wasn't going to sit by idly and allow her publisher to tarnish his name.

His gaze strayed to her trembling lips. "I'm hurt that you think so poorly of me. Why would I ever do that to you? I'm a professional journalist, not some hack."

Judah scoffed. "I've asked myself the same question about a lot of people here in Serenity Peak over the last four years. I reached the conclusion that there aren't always good reasons for human behavior." Judah could hear the bitterness ringing out in his voice. When had he let it consume him so wholeheartedly? Had losing Mary and Zane forever hardened him?

Autumn shook her head, causing her light brown hair streaked with gold to swirl around her shoulders. "You know me, Judah. Or at least you used to. That's not my style."

Judah wished he could believe her. So many years stood between them. Time hadn't stood still. It seemed as if they'd lived a lifetime without one another. In many ways they were strangers.

"We don't know each other any longer. Not really," Judah said. Just saying the words out loud caused a little hitch in his heart. Never in a million years had he ever imagined they would be living such separate lives. If anyone had asked him back then, Judah would have predicted they'd be married and raising a house full of kids together. He shoved the thought down. It was incredibly disloyal of him to even think such a thing when his life had revolved around Zane and Mary.

Autumn's expression crumpled. She frowned at him. "I don't believe you can ever truly stop knowing someone you were once close to the way we were. And it might sound strange, but I'd like to think we can still be friends. I'm back for good, Judah. We're going to be in each other's orbit."

A ragged sigh slipped past his lips. "Maybe not. I don't get out much these days. I tend to stick to my own company."

"Sean mentioned that to me." She bit her lip. "Judah, it might not be any of my business, but you were always such a big part of the Serenity Peak community. The Judah I used to know was woven into the fabric of our hometown. He wasn't antisocial. Or angry. You were a leader in every facet of this town."

Judah bristled. Clearly Autumn didn't understand what he'd been through. The accident had forever changed him. He no longer cared about being at the center of all the goings-on in Serenity Peak. Too much hurt rested on his heart. But what did she know about it? Autumn hadn't lived in town for ages. She hadn't lived through tragedy as he had.

"You're right. It really isn't any of your business. I'm sorry I don't measure up to the younger version of myself." Anger vibrated in his voice.

Autumn's jaw dropped, and before she could say another word, Judah turned on his heels and strode toward his truck. He revved the engine and took off with a roar, letting his vehicle get the last word in. Even though he told himself not to do it, Judah looked in his rearview mirror to get a final glimpse of Autumn. Something tugged at his heart at the sight of her standing in the same spot where he'd left her. Her gaze trailed after him, her arms folded stiffly across her chest.

He swallowed past the bile rising up in his throat. Why had he been so curt with her? So mean and short-tempered? What was it about Autumn that always left him wrestling with a host of emotions he would rather not face? Judah quickly looked away from her and focused on the road up ahead.

She had pricked at something inside of him he'd been struggling with for the past four years when he'd lost his family. Autumn's words had reminded him that he hadn't always been this way. He'd been kinder and gentler. A huge question came into sharp focus. Where had the old Judah gone and would he ever find his way back to the man he'd once been?

Dear Lord. Give me strength. Autumn repeated the words over and over again after she headed back inside Northern Lights. She'd almost followed after Judah to give him a piece of her mind for being so rude to her. *Mind her business!* He'd acted as if she was a nosy town busybody instead of a concerned friend. She let out a sigh. Not that he considered her a friend anymore. Judah had made that simple fact perfectly clear. Tears pricked her eyes and she furiously blinked them away. Although she'd fallen out of love with him many years ago, she still cared about him. Seeing him so broken caused an ache inside her chest. It was part of her nature to be a problem solver. She hadn't meant any harm.

As she walked into her brother's office to gather her purse and coat, Autumn noticed Sean sitting back at his desk talking on the phone. Seconds later he ended his conversation, quickly turning his attention in her direction.

"Are you okay?" Sean asked as he scanned her face.

Autumn let out an indelicate snort. "I thought you didn't want to get involved."

Sean rolled his eyes. "I don't, but I can still check on my baby sister can't I?"

"I guess," she said in a low voice. Her conversation with Judah had been full of tension and she had no idea how to shrug it off. Being at odds with people always left her unsettled. It would take her a bit of time to calm herself down.

"Don't take this the wrong way, but you look as if you were whirled around by a tornado. What happened?" Sean asked.

Autumn placed her hands by her hips. "I don't know how you and Judah are best friends," she exploded. "He has a huge chip on his shoulder and he seems to think everyone in Serenity Peak is out to get him, including yours truly. I just came back to town and he's acting as if I have an axe to grind with him."

Sean rubbed his temple. "That's about right. Try not to get too upset about Judah." Sean made a face. "He's really been through a lot, Autumn. Losing Mary was bad enough, but his only child as well. Zane was his mini me. That nearly killed him." Sean made a hissing sound. "And these whispers about Fishful Thinking being part of the fraud probe are tearing him apart. He won't admit it, but I can tell. He tries to be strong, but I can see the fault lines."

Autumn nodded. All of the anger she was holding onto began to dissipate. Judah had suffered major trauma. Of course he was bitter and angry. Who could blame him for wanting some distance from the townsfolk? Or brooding over his losses? She felt a bit ashamed that she hadn't been more sensitive. The interaction between them was complicated by their history. She should have known better than to try to give him advice, even though it had been well-meaning.

"I wasn't here when the accident happened, but I can imagine how devastating it must've been," Autumn said. "The truth is, Judah and I don't know each other anymore. I said some things that he most likely viewed as overstepping." She shrugged. "I should have kept my mouth shut."

Sean quirked his mouth. "These days it doesn't take much to rattle him. Maybe you should just steer clear of Judah." He jutted his chin in the direction of her belly. "Your focus should be squarely on my niece or nephew."

"I can't argue with you about that." She rubbed her palm over her stomach in the hopes she would feel some movement. "I'm going to drive over to Sugar Works to see Violet." Autumn took a quick glance at her watch. "She's expecting me shortly." Just the thought of seeing her close friend after such a long time apart almost made her forget about Judah's bad attitude.

Sean smiled, showcasing a sweet set of dimples. "That'll be good for you. You won't believe all the changes over there."

Autumn grinned at her brother. "I can't wait to see," she exclaimed, waving as she exited the room. Paying a visit to Violet and the birch syrup company would serve as a perfect distraction from her run-in with Judah. She had to face facts. He wasn't the man she'd once known and loved. Time and circumstances had forever changed him.

Love and light was her new motto. With a baby on the way and a new life to build in Serenity Peak, Autumn had to focus on those things. If she did well with this story on the local fishing industry, the *Tribune* might keep her on their payroll long-term. That would mean that she would be able to support herself and the baby. Although her ex had offered her child support, she didn't want to solely rely on those funds. She was determined to show her child that she could stand on her own two feet and make a good life for them in Alaska.

Fifteen minutes later, Autumn was approaching the turnoff on the road that led to Sugar Works. The gold and cream sign surrounded by birch trees and snow was graceful and beautiful.

Serenity Peak was a town that had been formed as a haven for people seeking peace and refuge from their troubles. As a result, many of the local businesses centered around wellness and artistic endeavors. Sugar Works specialized in creating all-natural birch syrup that was low in sugar and additives. The company had become so popular that the family had branched out to gift baskets and self-care items sold in a store on the property. From what Autumn gleaned from her conversations with Violet, Sugar Works was one of the most profitable companies in Alaska. The business employed a large number of locals, which energized the local economy.

Autumn navigated her truck toward the two-story log-style home. A feeling of nostalgia washed over her. This house was as familiar to her as her own. She'd spent countless hours here hanging out with her best friend. The Drummonds had always been welcoming and kind to her. As soon as she stepped down from the truck, she spotted Violet striding toward her and wildly waving her arms.

"Autumn!" Violet called out as she came rushing toward her with arms extended in greeting.

"Vi!" Autumn said as Violet enveloped her in a welcoming hug. A lemony scent rose to her nostrils. Violet's long hair brushed across her cheek. Autumn didn't ever want to stop embracing her best friend.

When they finally pulled apart, Violet reached for her hands and took a step back. "Let me get a good look at you." She began nodding her head and smiling. "You look fantastic. Other than a little bit of a baby belly, you're the same as always. Pregnancy really suits you."

Autumn grinned. "I haven't even dealt with morning sickness. How about that?"

"You're blessed. When I was pregnant with Chase I couldn't keep a thing down. It made for a pretty miserable nine months, but I wouldn't trade him for anything in this world."

"Of course you wouldn't. He's a keeper," Autumn said. "Is he around? I'd love to give him a hug." Chase was Violet's only child. At nine years old, he was a warm-hearted, decent kid who'd always been close with his mom. The only static between the two had revolved around Chase never knowing his father. To this day, even Autumn wasn't privy to all the details about Violet's relationship with Chase's father or why his identity was such a closely held secret.

"He's over in Kodiak with some friends for a birthday getaway. He'll be back in a few days though." She shoved her hands in her jean pockets. "I'm trying to give him some freedom since he always accuses me of being a helicopter mom."

"You're a great Mom, Violet. If I'm half as devoted as you are my child will be quite fortunate."

Violet fanned her face with her hand. "You're going to make me cry. Now, how are you getting acclimated to Serenity Peak? It's been a minute since you lived here."

"So far so good, except I had a slight run-in with Judah at Northern Lights. He overheard me talking to Sean about my *Tribune* piece and he got really heated. For some reason, he assumed I was going to link him with the fraud allegations swirling around," Autumn explained.

Violet ran a hand through her strawberry blond hair and made a tutting sound. "It's a shame the two of you are at odds. If you're writing a piece about the local fishing industry, there's no one who can better assist you than Judah. That guy knows his stuff."

Violet was right. Judah was a fourth generation Alaskan fisherman. He'd come out of the womb knowing the ins and outs of the industry. If things weren't so strained between them Autumn wouldn't think twice about asking. But after their run-in she wasn't sure if he would be receptive to helping her.

"I don't know, Vi. He wasn't giving out good vibes, if I'm being perfectly honest. Once he found out I was working with the *Tribune*, he got really heated." She chewed on her lip. "Anyway, wouldn't it be a conflict of interest to get help from someone who might be implicated in the investigation?"

"You're an ethical person, Autumn. And so is he. He's innocent until proven guilty. I have no doubt that if you uncovered something shady, you wouldn't bury it."

Autumn shook her head. "No, I couldn't ever do that. Not even for Judah."

Violet locked gazes with Autumn, and although no words were exchanged between them, Autumn knew her friend understood. She had been an up close and personal witness to Autumn's love story with Judah. More than anyone else, Violet knew how difficult it had been to end their relationship.

"How's Skye doing?" Autumn asked, swiftly changing the subject. She had no desire to dwell on the situation. As a journalist, she needed to figure out a way to make the research angle work so her article was stellar.

"She's okay," Violet answered. "It's taken her a long time to move past what happened with Tyler." Violet clenched her jaw. "For the first year she was miserable, so it's nice to see she's emerging from the fog of depression."

Autumn's stomach lurched. She hadn't realized how bad things had been for Skye and it made her feel guilty for not being in Serenity Peak to help. "I can't imagine how difficult that was for her. She built her whole life around him and the idea of becoming his wife." Autumn watched as her best friend blinked back tears.

Autumn placed her arm around Violet and pulled her close to her side. Due to the ten-year age gap between the two sisters and the loss of their mother when they were young, Violet had served as Skye's surrogate mom. They'd always been exceptionally close.

"So, are you still writing an article about this place?" Violet asked, gesturing with her arm toward the expanse of land where the birch trees grew. "I've been looking forward to it ever since you mentioned it. Sugar Works has been doing well, but media attention is always a good thing."

"Of course I am. Not only was I eager to lay eyes on you, but I have my camera with me to take some pics to go along with my article." Autumn patted the camera bag she'd strapped over her shoulder. The idea of capturing Sugar Works for a lifestyle feature was exciting.

Violet clapped her hands together and grinned. "Well

then let me show you what's new. A lot has changed here in the last two years."

Autumn let out a low whistle as she looked around the property. "I knew Sugar Works was doing well, but you've really expanded your operations." She spotted a few new buildings in the distance. Violet looped her arm through Autumn's as they headed toward a small structure with several cars parked in front and people walking around. A sign reading "Sugar's Place" hung from the porch awning. A sweet bright green rocking chair sat near the entrance.

"This is our general store, named in Mama's honor. Come on inside and check it out," Violet said.

Sugar Drummond, Violet's mother, had been the heart and soul of the family. A random bout with the flu had led to her sudden death eleven years ago. Loving and lively, Sugar had conceived the idea for Sugar Works years before she passed away. Her husband, Abel, got it up and running in her memory. Sadly, Sugar hadn't been around to savor the success of the wildly popular birch syrup company.

Once Autumn stepped inside the shop she was immersed in the down-home vibe of the establishment. A vintage Welcome to Alaska sign hung by the entrance. The smell of birch syrup and lavender permeated the space. Beautiful items were displayed in every nook and cranny. A vase of forget-me-nots sat at the checkout desk.

"You've outdone yourselves," Autumn gushed. "This place has so much charm."

"Thanks," Violet said with a grin. "I think Mama would be proud."

"Of course she would," Autumn said as she picked up a lavender sachet and raised it to her nose.

"Autumn!" Skye raced toward Autumn. Just before she reached her, Violet stepped between them.

"Easy there, sis. Baby on board," Violet cautioned. "You were coming at her like a runaway train."

"I'm sorry," Skye said, appearing sheepish. "You know me. I always get a little carried away."

"But your heart's always in the right place. I'm excited to see you too," Autumn said, leaning down and pressing a kiss on Skye's temple.

Skye, with a mane of curly blond hair and big blue eyes, had always been the town charmer, ever since she was a little girl. Although she had a reputation for being spoiled, Autumn knew that her loved ones had only been trying to fill the void left by her mother's death. Perhaps they'd gone overboard, but Autumn believed in Skye's potential.

"Daddy's coming right behind me," Skye said with a wide smile. "He's even more excited than I am if that's possible."

Within seconds Abel appeared—a big bear of a man with a long grizzled beard and small spectacles that didn't seem to fit his round face. He'd always been a larger-than-life figure in Serenity Peak. Autumn loved him like a favorite uncle. With an ambling gait he came over and clasped her hands in his. "Welcome back, sunshine. It's been a long time coming."

She blinked back tears as Violet, Skye and Abel fussed over her. Being with the Drummonds was a second homecoming for Autumn. This wonderful sense of community was a huge reason why she had chosen to move back home and raise her baby here. New York had been vibrant and pulsing with life, but it had never felt like a warm embrace. Not like Serenity Peak where she was woven into the fabric of the town.

Autumn snapped photos and jotted down notes while getting a tour of the renovated property. After saying her goodbyes she began the drive back to Cecily's place. The idea of getting assistance from Judah continued to flit through her mind as she drove the scenic route that gave her stunning views of the mountains. Just because it might be awkward to ask for his help didn't mean she shouldn't do it, Autumn reckoned.

Making a good impression with the *Alaskan Tribune* was vital to her long-term employment here in Alaska and she was struggling to flesh out this piece. Supposedly there was a federal investigation going on, but she hadn't found any information regarding it.

There were no lengths she wouldn't go to in order to provide for this baby. All she wanted to do was bring her child into the world and provide a wonderful life for the both of them.

Autumn was going to reach out to Judah and offer him an olive branch in the hopes of getting his assistance on her article. Things weren't going as she had expected. She couldn't deny it would be tricky to get Judah to agree. Being around Judah had a way of making Autumn think about things she'd put in her rear-view mirror ages ago.

She couldn't allow herself to get consumed by Judah and all of his issues, even if a part of her longed to help him heal.

Chapter Five

A few days after Judah had butted heads with Autumn at Northern Lights, he was at home working in his yard. The previous night's flurry had yielded a few more feet of snow in an already wintry February. For Judah, the crack of dawn usually signified an early departure from the marina for Fishful Thinking and its crew. Heading out on the Bay in the wee hours of the morning always reaped the best rewards. Since it was Sunday he'd been able to sleep in this morning, which was an unusual treat for a fisherman.

Even though Judah no longer considered himself a man of faith, he had arranged to shut down operations on the Lord's day so his crew could worship and spend precious time with their families. Sunday had always been one of his favorite days to hang out with Zane and attend services together as a family. Even though he didn't worship any longer, it didn't mean others couldn't. If they wanted to waste their time in church, who was he to argue? All he knew for certain was that God had abandoned him in his darkest hour.

The sound of crunching tires on the snowy ground drew his attention to the tree-covered lane leading to his property. Someone was turning in to his driveway. These days Judah didn't get many visitors out here with the exception of a handful of folks he could still tolerate. Sean, Brody and his nephew, Ryan. Even Leif had stopped coming around since they had reached an impasse with Judah refusing to listen to his brother's side of the story, and Leif not apologizing for being disloyal. Judah had gone over it so many times in his head, but he still couldn't reconcile the fact that his brother still associated with some of the town residents who spread the rumors about Mary being under the influence at the time of the accident. It served as yet another devastating blow.

Sean's red truck came into view. He could see Autumn's face as she steered the vehicle toward him. He would know the graceful tilt of her head anywhere, combined with her sun-kissed brown hair and striking features. After all this time she was still indelibly imprinted on him even though more than a decade stood between them.

What was she doing here? He battled against a feeling of irritation. He didn't feel like dealing with people today. Especially Autumn. She had a way of getting under his skin and burrowing there. That knowledge wrecked him. He couldn't even allow his mind to go there.

"Hey there, Judah," Autumn called out as she shut the truck door and made her way toward him. In her berry-colored parka and jeans, he barely noticed her baby bump. Autumn's athletic physique hid her pregnancy from casual observers. In her high school days, she'd played basketball and soccer, leading her team to championships in both sports.

"Autumn," Judah said, putting his shovel down. "What brings you out here?"

"A peace offering," Autumn said, holding up a small basket overflowing with items. "I didn't like the way we left things the other day. It didn't sit well with me."

"Thanks, but it wasn't necessary to bring me anything," he said, taking the basket off her hands. It was filled with all kinds of treats—hot chocolate, scones, muffins and birch syrup. The aroma of the baked goods caused his stomach to grumble. He looked up at Autumn. "Did you bake these yourself?" he asked. Judah felt a smirk tugging at his lips. Autumn had never been a baker. Maybe now with the baby coming she'd been honing her culinary skills.

"I sure did," she said with a huge smile. "Not to brag, but I'm a pretty good baker these days. I took some lessons from a semi-famous New York baker and learned the craft." Autumn was beaming so hard Judah didn't have the heart to make any jokes. The image of Autumn baking up a storm in a trendy New York City loft apartment flitted through his mind. Her life, he imagined, had been very different than the one he'd led in small town Alaska. Miles apart from the one they had dreamed about living as a couple.

"Well, if they smell as good as they taste, I'm in for a treat," Judah said, surprising himself with his civility. His dad had always said Autumn brought out his sweet side. Judah was far more content these days being reserved.

Autumn shoved her mittened hands inside her jacket pockets. "Judah, do you think we could talk? I have something to ask you."

Judah raised a brow. He was on high alert now and a bit annoyed. Of course Autumn hadn't just swung by to make nice with him. Something else was on her agenda. He let out a little huff of air as a feeling of disappointment swept over him.

"What is it?" he asked. "You don't need to beat around the bush. Just spit it out."

Autumn planted her hands on her hips. "And you don't need to be so gruff with me."

For a few beats they simply stared at one another, neither one giving an inch. It reminded him of the past and the numerous times they'd butted heads with one another. Neither one of them had ever wanted to give in to the other due to their strong wills. Each and every time they had ended up laughing it off and repairing the situation with a tender kiss. Something inside of Judah slightly softened. The ties he shared with Autumn always seemed to rise to the surface even when he tried to stuff the memories down. She wasn't like anybody else in Serenity Peak, so he had to make concessions for that fact.

"It's pretty cold out here. Why don't you come inside and I'll make us some of this hot cocoa?" he suggested. Although he knew Autumn was a capable woman, Judah felt protective of her. *Old habits were hard to break,* he thought.

Autumn shivered and crossed her arms around her chest. "Don't mind if I do. It's downright frosty today. One thing I haven't quite missed about Alaska is being chilled to the bone."

"Watch your step," he instructed, reaching for her elbow as they walked across a slick patch of snow. He made a hissing sound. "I need to put more salt down on this ice." Judah reached into the big bucket by the side of the house and retrieved a cup full of salt that he sprinkled over the ice.

He wasn't going to have Autumn fall. Not on his watch. She was carrying precious cargo.

Once they made their way inside, Judah headed toward the kitchen and set the basket down on the counter. He put the kettle on then turned back to Autumn. "Make yourself comfortable. I can get a cushion if you need one."

Autumn chuckled. The rich sound of her laughter filled up his kitchen. "I'm good, Judah. Hopefully I won't need any cushions until I'm in my final stretch."

Pregnancy was treating her well, he thought. She looked like pure sunshine.

"Just making sure," he said, reaching into his cabinet to pull out mugs. When the kettle squealed Judah began filling the cups with cocoa then pouring hot water and milk on to the powder. He placed a mug and a spoon in front of Autumn then slid into a chair.

A feeling of nostalgia gripped him as he stirred the cocoa. "You never met my son, but he loved hot chocolate. He once drank so much of it on Christmas Eve he stayed up half the night with a bellyache." Judah surprised himself by laughing at his recollection of Zane. Words couldn't describe the ache of missing his beautiful boy.

"I actually saw him on one of my visits home. The two of you were going into the five-and-dime on Main Street. I should have said hello, but—" her voice trailed off.

"I get it," he said, bringing his mug to his lips. He didn't say it to Autumn, but he wasn't sure that he would have stopped to talk to her either if he'd spotted her. Especially if Mary had been present. His wife had always been a bit jealous of what he and Autumn had shared. Judah had never been able to fully convince her that Autumn was his past while she was his future.

"It made my heart soar to see the two of you together. You seemed like such a natural at fatherhood. Your body language and the way he was gazing up at you spoke volumes." She fiddled with the rim of her mug. "I hope it's okay that I'm sharing this with you."

A thick lump sat in his throat and he coughed to try and clear it. "It's okay," he conceded. "I try not to think about him too often, but at moments like this his presence looms large."

Autumn looked at him with wide eyes. He sensed she wanted to say something but was biting her tongue. Folks tiptoed around him a lot, so he easily recognized the signs.

"What?" he asked. "You don't need to hold back with me. I don't break easily." Otherwise he would have shattered by this point, he wanted to add.

She locked eyes with him across the table. Her gaze felt so intense Judah was tempted to look away.

"I can't imagine how hard it's been for you to mourn the loss of your family, but I'm sure you have so many beautiful memories of Zane." Her tone oozed compassion. "If you let them, those thoughts will nurture you. I know it's not the same, but when my Gran passed away I had so many keepsakes to remind me of how much she loved me." She looked around her. "I noticed you don't have any pictures of your son or Mary hanging up."

Judah put his mug down on the table and took a calming breath. Autumn no doubt meant well but Judah knew pictures wouldn't ease the sting of all he'd lost. What good would it do other than torment him? Their faces were already imprinted on his soul. Wasn't that enough?

"Someone once told me that there's no one way to grieve. This is my way. I don't like visual reminders." He stirred his drink. "I don't know if it's the healthiest way to deal with it, but it's the path I've chosen to walk."

Autumn seemed chastened. "I'm sorry," she blurted out. "It's not my place to tell you how to mourn."

Judah didn't correct her. He'd gotten a lot of advice over the years. All it did was make him wish he could just burrow inside his house and never leave. In the space of four years he'd lost Zane, his father and Mary. A triple kick in the gut. Even now, as he was emerging from the darkest recesses of loss, he still wondered why God had let it all happen.

"So…you said that you swung by to ask me something? I think you've kept me in suspense long enough." He looked at Autumn over the rim of his mug as he finished the dregs of his cocoa.

Autumn nodded her head as long strands of her hair swirled around her shoulders. It was hard for him not to notice everything about her—the graceful slope of her neck, her fully rosy lips and the little freckles dotting her cheeks. She drummed her fingers on the table and bit her lip. His stomach did a little flip. He knew the signs of nervousness in Autumn.

"I need your help, Judah, with my article. I've wracked my brain and you're honestly the only one who can help me out. Please say yes. My future in Serenity Peak is riding on this story!"

Judah's expression reflected shock and a fair amount of dismay. Autumn held up her hands before he could respond and shoot her idea down. Some instinct warned her that he wasn't going to agree to help her. "Just hear me out. You're an expert in the field, Judah. An authentic Alaskan fisherman. So much is at stake. I need to knock this assignment out of the park and I'm already feeling a bit in over my head."

She was beginning to ramble. Asking for this huge favor after all their years apart was humbling and a bit pushy. At times she wasn't even sure if she knew the man sitting across from her. Tragedy had forever altered his life. Perhaps this really wasn't a good idea even if she was desperate.

"I know this might seem awkward because of our past—" she began.

"That's not a factor," he snapped, cutting her off. "Our relationship was over a long time ago. We've both moved on with our lives."

"So you'll help me?" she asked. A sense of relief swept over her. If she couldn't deliver this article, she might be let go. In her situation as a single soon-to-be mother, stable employment was a huge factor in her ability to start over in Alaska.

"I didn't say that," he said, sighing. "What kind of help are you talking about?" Judah asked, furrowing his brows.

"To be honest, I'm a bit in over my head. I'm hitting a few brick walls with setting up interviews with local fishermen and the clock is ticking," she admitted, feeling sheepish. She'd never been so frustrated in her professional life. It felt as if she was spending all her time chasing down folks who didn't want to talk to her. This assignment was proving to be way more challenging than she'd imagined.

"Meaning?" Judah pressed. He sat back in his chair and folded his arms across his chest.

Her shoulders slumped. "No one seems interested in talking to me, and I have a deadline looming. Doors are literally being slammed in my face. I guess twelve years away from my hometown makes me a stranger."

"That's not surprising, Autumn. You've been away from Serenity Peak for a long time. Don't take this the wrong way, but I'm sure they're wondering if you can be trusted." He let out a brittle laugh. "Folks in the fishing industry don't want to get tangled up in a federal investigation or say the wrong thing on the record. And I can't say that I blame them," he muttered.

"First of all, the article is a three-part series. The focus of my work isn't solely on the allegations of fraud.

I'm determined to write about local fishermen and how they've shaped Alaska. But I need to speak with actual fishermen to pull this off. You could make those introductions for me, Judah. You're very well respected in your industry," Autumn said. "And if you could take me out on your vessel just so I can understand the mechanics of how it all works with reporting the catch, I'd be ever so grateful." She knew it might seem pushy, but she figured she'd go all out. The worst he could do was say no, which at this moment seemed quite possible.

Judah ran a hand over his face. She could tell he was thinking things over.

"I'll make a few calls and see who I can reel in," he conceded. "No pun intended." She let out a little whoop of excitement.

He held up his hand. "Don't get too revved up just yet. There are a few folks I don't get along with so you might have to make those contacts on your own. But if my friends come through, you'll definitely have enough to write an article or two." The frown etched on his face hinted at things Autumn didn't dare ask about. From the sounds of it, Judah wasn't on good terms with a number of Serenity Peak residents. She had thought that the fishing community was an exception.

Autumn stood up from her chair. "Well, I'm going to dash before you change your mind." Judah walked with her to the door. She reached for her parka on the hook and put it on before sliding her feet into her comfy winter boots, then turned back toward him.

As gratitude bubbled up inside of her, Autumn threw herself against Judah's chest and wrapped her arms around him. A woodsy scent rose to her nostrils. For a moment she felt transported to a place and time when she'd felt safe and protected in his arms. After a few seconds she released him, immediately noticing the tension on his face. Regret washed over her. She'd acted on impulse and created a terribly awkward situation between them. Judah's body language was stiff and uncomfortable. Clearly, she had crossed a line with him.

Why was it so difficult for her to accept that time had altered their once close relationship? And she didn't mean romance. They had been friends well before they'd fallen in love. A strong foundation of friendship had paved the way for a tender romance.

"Well, thanks again," she said lamely, beating a fast path out of the house. A fierce wind whipped across her face as she made her way back to the truck. Frankly, she needed the chill to cool her heated cheeks. Embarrassment threatened to swallow her up whole.

When she got behind the wheel she paused for a moment to cover her face with her hands. *Why had she hugged him?* It had been a rash and foolish act. She'd been so relieved to know he'd be helping her that she'd fallen into old familiar rhythms. Those days were over and done with.

Now she felt all turned upside down. She hadn't expected to feel such a rush of nostalgia. Being in close proximity with him had sparked something inside of her that she needed to snuff out as quickly as possible. Maybe it was a terrible idea to have asked for his assistance. It meant they would be thrown into one another's path.

Get a grip! she scolded herself. You're not a moon-eyed twentysomething anymore.

Autumn had come back to Serenity Peak with a single-minded purpose. Everything in her new life revolved around creating a solid foundation for her precious child and ensuring that she had the ability to put bread on the table. She harbored dreams of buying her own home for the two of them. She couldn't live with her sister indefinitely. And she wasn't going to take her eyes off the prize by getting distracted by Judah Campbell. He was grappling with his own serious issues.

Even though it had been twelve years since they had been a couple, Autumn couldn't ignore the sudden rush she'd experienced in those few moments back at his house. It served as a reminder that she needed to keep a professional distance between herself and Judah.

Judah watched from his front window as Autumn drove down the lane and out of his sight. Her unexpected visit had been full of surprises. He began performing his breathing exercises in order to calm down his rapidly beating heart. He'd been holding on fairly well until she'd sucker punched him with an out of the blue hug. Having Autumn pressed up against his chest had thrown him completely off-kilter.

He couldn't think of the last time he'd had such close physical contact with anyone. Part of being removed from the social whirl in Serenity Peak meant he wasn't shaking hands or sharing hugs with the residents. Judah hadn't missed the close contact with human beings until a few minutes ago. Everything about Autumn's nearness had awoken his senses. The lemony scent of her shampoo, the softness of her hair and the way the top of her head skimmed his chin.

And he had almost said no to her request. The words had been on the tip of his tongue when something inside him reversed course. She had a baby to raise and it wouldn't be much trouble to smooth the path for her with his fishermen friends. Taking her out on his boat might be a tad more difficult. Judah really didn't want that type of closeness to Autumn. As he'd just learned, that's how things could easily go astray.

Ever since he'd first seen Autumn at the pier, thoughts of her had permeated his waking hours. And perhaps some of his dreams as well. Thinking about her and their past relationship made him feel incredibly disloyal to Mary. His wife had loved him with such unbridled devotion. And he'd loved her in return—in a different way than he had loved Autumn, but it had been real and strong nevertheless. Autumn Hines had always had a hold on him. She had shattered his heart once before and left him gutted.

Only a fool would go back down that road again.

Chapter Six

"Are you sure it's a good idea to work with Judah? That just seems like you're asking for trouble." Her brother was looking at her with a mix of surprise and concern. They were standing in Northern Light's kitchen as Sean packed up meals for senior citizens in town. It was his way of giving back to a community that had always sustained him. "From what I saw the other day, the two of you are bound to clash."

"I'm hoping it'll be okay," Autumn said. "I've made dozens of calls for interviews and so far, no one has called me back. Hopefully that'll change when Judah gives me his personal contacts." She wrinkled her nose. "Otherwise my assignment might not even get off the ground. I need to make this work."

She wasn't going to admit to Sean that she was thinking along the same lines about Judah. It hadn't escaped her notice that her ex-boyfriend was a bit all over the place. At times she saw flashes of the man she had once known, but those instances were few and far between.

Autumn had to believe he was simply trying to read-just himself after the trauma of the accident. She was willing to extend him grace.

"Don't say that I didn't warn you. I love him like a brother, but he's not the guy you remember. He's difficult." To her ears, Sean sounded judgmental.

"It's understandable," she snapped. "He's been through unimaginable trauma."

Her words crackled in the air between them. Sean raised a brow as he gazed at her. She instantly felt badly about her tone. She wasn't sure why the thought of Judah being criticized made her so prickly.

"I know, bug. I was here," Sean responded in a low voice. "I've seen him through some dark days. I'm team Judah 24/7. But I have to be honest, especially with my little sister."

She reached out and placed her arm around his waist. "I'm sorry, Sean. I don't know where that came from." He looked down at her with an all-knowing expression. She had the feeling he was biting his tongue. Autumn didn't have to guess what Sean might have wanted to say. He no doubt thought she was sticking up for Judah because of what he'd once meant to her.

"Switching gears, could you run these meals out to Ida? I'm headed in the other direction of town with these additional food deliveries so you would be doing me a giant favor."

"Of course. It would be my pleasure. Miss Ida is my favorite teacher of all time." Ida Mayweather had taught fourth grade in Serenity Peak for over forty-two years. She was beloved by all. A recent health condition had left her unable to drive and housebound. Sean made sure to send over food on a regular basis as well as groceries.

Autumn bagged up Ida's meals and headed outside to the lot. Once she was in the vehicle she turned the radio on and began singing along to her favorite ballads. Some of these songs she hadn't heard in years. What a nice feeling to be able to enjoy the simple pleasures of life. With the end of her marriage, her husband's infidelity and this move back to Alaska, Autumn's stress level had been incredibly high.

Miss Ida lived out by the mountains near the famous Serenity Peak hot springs. The hot springs were a hidden gem in town. Its natural beauty was unmarred by any type of construction or developments. Pure, unspoiled Alaskan land. When Autumn had been a teenager, going swimming in the hot springs on the coldest day of the year had been a rite of passage.

When she reached the moose crossing sign, Autumn steered the truck off the main road and drove down a snow-packed lane. There weren't any neighboring houses for at least a mile, which made her worry about Miss Ida's safety. What if she fell or a fire started in her kitchen? Would anyone be near enough to help her in time?

Once she spotted the Welcome to Ida's Place sign hung on an ancient white spruce tree, Autumn knew she had arrived at her destination. It had been ages since she'd come all the way out here. A sweet memory washed over her as she stepped out of the truck and gazed across the property. Autumn and her classmates had once been invited to an end-of-the-year picnic at

Miss Ida's house. To this day she could still remember the chocolate cake and the gaily decorated picnic tables in her yard, as well as the excitement flowing amongst her peers.

The sight of Ida's house peeking through the trees caused the corners of Autumn's mouth to turn upward in a gigantic smile. The powder pink color was unusual for Alaska, but it was pure Ida. The home was cozy and unique. She had once famously said, "You don't get anything in life by being a cookie cutout of everyone else."

She walked up to the house and gently knocked on the front door, admiring the beautiful wreath with dried bluebonnets laced with baby's breath. Miss Ida had always been wonderful with crafts and making beauty out of ordinary objects. When the door swung open, Autumn had to stop herself from letting out a gasp. Judah was standing in the doorway looking very at home. He was laughing about something, and for a moment, there was a glimmer of the old Judah. His handsome features and straight white teeth were on full display. She wondered if she should retreat. Clearly, she was walking in on a tender moment between Judah and Ida that she didn't want to spoil.

"Who's at the door?" Miss Ida called out from behind him.

"It's Autumn. Autumn Hines," Judah answered, his gaze never straying from her own.

"I just came to bring Miss Ida some meals from Northern Lights," Autumn explained in a low voice, pressing the bag against his chest. When she tried to turn around and leave, Judah reached out and lightly grabbed her arm. He turned her right back around to face him.

"Where do you think you're going? Ida would have a fit if I let you leave." A hint of a smile rested on his lips. "And I would get the blame."

"Don't stand on ceremony. Let the girl in," Ida barked from inside.

"The queen has spoken." Judah shook his head and waved her inside, quickly closing the door behind her. At this point she knew better than to argue with the Queen Bee. After quickly shedding her winter parka and boots, Judah led her into the adjoining room.

As soon as she stepped into the living room, Miss Ida came into view. She was sitting in a love seat with a crocheted blanket draped over her torso and legs. She was wearing a pretty green sweater dress. With small spectacles, a heart-shaped face and a head full of gray hair, she hadn't changed all that much. Just a few more lines on her lovely face. As always, she was adorable. Delilah was laying down next to Ida's chair, looking like a pampered pooch.

A fire crackled in the fireplace, providing a sharp contrast to the frigid temperature outdoors. Warmth immediately enveloped her as soon as she'd crossed the threshold.

"Miss Ida!" Autumn flew to her former teacher's side and bent down to give her a tight hug. The scent of eucalyptus rose to her nostrils, bringing back another wave of memories.

"Autumn, I think it's high time you stopped calling

me Miss Ida. Just Ida from now on," she said, wagging her finger at her. "We're all grown folks now."

"Will do," Autumn said sheepishly. Judah was looking on with interest. He was practically smiling! If Ida was responsible for his lighthearted mood, then she was all in favor of them hanging out together on a regular basis.

"Oh, it's been a long time," Ida said, dabbing at her eyes with her finger. "I've missed you. And from what I hear from Sean, you're expecting a baby. Isn't that wonderful?"

"I am," Autumn said, placing her hand on her belly. Although he didn't utter a word, Judah's eyes were trained on her stomach. *What was he thinking?* she wondered. About his own son who was no longer here? She couldn't imagine the painful road he'd walked.

"Bless you and this baby," Ida said. "Don't tell anyone, but the two of you were among my favorite students."

"No big surprise there," Judah said. "I always knew it," he said, snapping his fingers.

"Oh, you're still incorrigible," Ida said, her tinkling laughter filling the small space.

"So, what brings you here, Judah? Just paying a social visit?" Autumn asked. She'd been trying to stifle her curiosity about his presence at Ida's house, but in the end she couldn't resist inquiring. Sean and Cecily had painted Judah as a near recluse.

"Ida and I have a longstanding date once a month when my schedule allows it. We have lunch or play a few rounds of Scrabble," Judah explained. He winked at the older woman. "On occasion she lets me win." Ida was looking over at Judah as if he'd hung the moon.

And here Autumn had been under the impression that Judah only had a few friends in town. She considered it a good sign that he was branching out by regularly visiting Ida.

"I'm so blessed to have you making time to come see me," Ida said. She was gazing at Judah as if butter wouldn't melt in his mouth. "It gets lonely out here."

Autumn's felt a pang in her heart upon hearing her former teacher's words.

Judah reached out and lifted her hand up, pressing a kiss on her knuckles. "You know you're the only girl for me, Ida."

Ida gently swatted him with her hand. "Don't toy with me, Judah Campbell. You're still as charming as ever and twice as handsome. Isn't he, Autumn?"

Autumn shifted from one foot to the other. Ida meant well but she'd placed Autumn in a terribly awkward situation. "Yes," she admitted as a small sigh slipped past her lips. "He really is." She was telling the truth. Judah had always had an abundance of charm...and his good looks were obvious to any female with a pulse.

Judah looked over at her, and for a few moments their gazes locked and held. Something flickered between them that hummed in the air around them. Goosebumps pricked the back of her neck. She looked away after a few seconds, wondering if Ida had noticed anything. Perhaps she was imagining things. Nothing existed between her and Judah except their tangled past. And she didn't want anything either. All she dreamt about these days was holding a smiling baby in her arms.

"I was telling Judah how much I miss going fishing with my Clinton," Ida said with a sigh. "Those were the days." Clinton Mayweather hadn't been an Alaskan fisherman, but fishing had been a pastime that provided him with a great deal of happiness. Oftentimes he was accompanied by Ida when she wasn't in the classroom. They had shared a love story for the ages.

"He was such a sweetheart," Autumn said. Clinton had worked at the small post office in town, and he'd known everyone in Serenity Peak by name. Autumn smiled at the memory of the older man who had been short in stature but in possession of supersize charm.

"Any time you want to head out with me on Fishful Thinking, I'll be ready," Judah said, clasping his hand in hers.

"You're so kind, Judah. Always remember that weeping may endure for a night but joy cometh in the morning." Ida squeezed Judah's hand. "Be patient. I know you've been at rock bottom, but your joy is coming."

Judah didn't respond but simply nodded and patted Ida's hand. Autumn couldn't be sure, but she thought there was a sheen of moisture in his eyes.

Bless Ida. She had the best heart. Autumn hated to think that someone as lively and wonderful as Ida might be lonely in her everyday life. The older woman had so much to give the Serenity Peak community.

"Why don't we have some of my almond Bundt cake? It's one of my best recipes if I do say so myself. I can put a kettle on and make tea," Ida suggested.

"You don't have to ask me twice," Judah said, patting his stomach with extra emphasis.

Autumn knew she should be heading back to town to focus on work, but she couldn't resist Ida's invitation. It wasn't hard to see that the older woman was feeling a bit isolated and in need of company. "I never say no to cake," Autumn teased. Ida's face lit up, which caused a warm and fuzzy feeling to spread through Autumn's chest.

After heading to the kitchen where Judah slid the bag with Ida's meals into her fridge, Ida began cutting generous slices of the cake. As they settled down at the table, Autumn thought the kitchen had a serene ambiance. It reminded her of why she loved Serenity Peak so much. Ida had welcomed her back with open arms despite the fact that she'd been gone for twelve years. Watching Judah's rapport with Ida was the biggest revelation of all. Despite his traumas, he was still able to smile and be joyful. He was helping others. Trying to put one foot in front of the other.

As she bit into the almond cake, Autumn let out a sound of satisfaction as the mix of flavors hit her tongue. "This is delicious, Ida," she said. "If you ever get bored at home you could open up a bakery in town. Customers would be lining up outside the doors to experience this." She closed her eyes and savored the last morsel of the cake. When she opened them, Judah was looking over at her, his gaze intense.

"You think so?" Ida asked. Her tinkling laughter filled the air. "Clinton used to always tell me that he fell in love with my baked goods before he became smitten with me."

For the next half hour, they chatted recipes, baby names and discussed upcoming town events. The twenty-fifth annual town festival was coming up and Ida let it be known that she wouldn't miss it for the world. Judah didn't talk much but he listened intently, saying a few words here and there.

"I hate to eat and run," Autumn said, reluctantly standing up from the table, "but I've got to head out."

"Me too. I've got a delivery to make," Judah said, a regretful expression stamped on his face. "As always, I had a great time, Ida. I'll be back soon, way before you even have a chance to miss me."

"Not possible," Ida said with a sigh. "I miss you already."

After putting her coat and boots back on, Autumn said her goodbyes to Ida, again promising to come back to visit soon. Judah and Delilah trailed behind her as she stepped back outside into the cold.

"So, I've been in contact with a few buddies of mine. They're willing to talk to you and give you an overview of the problems we fishermen are facing these days." He shrugged. "Hopefully it will help. Most fishermen want to be featured in a positive light and have a spotlight shone on our endeavors."

Her heart leapt at the news. "Oh, Judah. That's wonderful. I really appreciate it." She was so relieved at Judah's announcement that she wanted to shout in celebration. Being a journalist meant the world to her and she would have been devastated if the assignment fell apart. It wouldn't bode too well for her standing with the *Tribune*.

"If you give me your cell number I can send them over as contacts."

"Sure thing," she said as she pulled out her cell phone and began exchanging information with him.

All of a sudden Autumn experienced a startling sensation in her stomach that caused her phone to slip from her hand to the ground. She let out a little cry and tightly gripped Judah's arm.

Judah became alarmed as soon as Autumn clutched him as if her life depended on it. The expression etched on her face was hard to read. Pain? Surprise? For the life of him, he wasn't sure what was going on but his pulse began to race.

"What's wrong?" he asked, fearing the worst. Because of what he had been through, Judah knew his mind often went to a worst-case scenario. He was still primed for disaster. Maybe he always would be.

"I'm sorry for grabbing you. I was just startled," she said, her eyes filled with wonder. "Oh, my stars. I—I think the baby just kicked me for the first time." She let out a shaky laugh. "It was the oddest feeling, but amazing at the same time."

She looked more radiant in this moment than he could ever remember. Joy lit her up like a beacon. He bent down and picked up her cell phone, quickly handing it back to her. It gave him a brief opportunity to catch his breath. He felt relief flow through him that she wasn't in harm's way. Of course she was excited. A baby's first movements were worthy of a celebration.

Autumn lovingly ran her hand over her abdomen. Judah couldn't quite manage to take his eyes off Autumn's perfectly rounded stomach. How many times had he placed his palm on Mary's stomach so he could feel Zane's kicks?

At this moment all he wanted to do was reach out and feel the baby kicking. It was such a beautiful affirmation of life. For so long now he had been almost afraid to live, scared of doing anything that might be viewed as enjoying himself or moving forward. Sean thought it was survivor's guilt. Maybe his best friend was right in his assessment? Lately he'd been taking baby steps toward finding a measure of happiness in his life. It was one of the reasons he enjoyed visiting Ida so much. She was restoring his faith in the residents of Serenity Peak.

"Go ahead. It's all right, Judah," Autumn prodded. "I don't mind." Autumn seemed to have read his thoughts. That's how it had always been between them. They had shared such a close bond, one he'd once thought of as unbreakable.

Judah tentatively reached out and placed his hand on her parka over her stomach. For a few moments they stood there waiting for something to happen. Disappointment flooded him at the idea that the moment might have passed. Then suddenly he felt movement under his hand. A thumping sensation began to pulse against his palm in rapid succession.

"Do you feel that?" Autumn asked, sounding breathless. Her eyes shimmered with happiness.

He nodded, not trusting himself to speak. A huge lump sat in his throat. At first the movements made him feel as if he was soaring high, until a feeling of such guilt washed over him it made him weak in the knees. This moment was too much to bear. A reminder of everything he'd lost.

What was he doing? This had absolutely no connection to him or his life.

It was pathetic to get so excited about a baby his ex-girlfriend was bringing into the world. He'd lost his only child. That knowledge would never change and it gutted him.

Judah needed to get away from here as fast as possible. Away from Autumn. Away from this celebratory moment. His emotions were all over the place right now. Grief had a way of working its way into a million different scenarios. Just when he thought he had turned a corner, the ache of loss had seized him by the throat and wouldn't let go.

"I need to make a fish delivery to Northern Lights. I've got to go." Judah forced the words out of his mouth, surprising himself by how steady his voice sounded. He turned away from Autumn, letting out a whistle so Delilah would follow him to the truck.

"Wait!" she called out after him. "What about my going out on Fishful Thinking with you and your crew?"

Judah wanted to let out a loud groan. Taking her out on his boat was the last thing he wanted to do, but he had always been a man of his word. He turned back toward her. "I'll give you a call so we can arrange something." The brilliant smile he received in return instantly made him regret agreeing to take Autumn out on the Bay. Being around her wasn't good for him. There was such a thing as feeling too much, which was what had happened when he'd touched her stomach. Stuffing his emotions down was much safer territory for him.

His hands trembled as he situated himself in the driver's seat and placed his hands on the steering wheel. At moments like this Judah had always been able to pray. For Grace. Mercy. Peace. Wisdom. Now, he couldn't even find the words. And even if he could, Judah wasn't sure God would be listening to him.

Autumn watched as Judah roared away from Ida's house with his truck's wheels spinning on the snow-covered ground. His desire to be as far as possible from her was obvious. She really didn't blame him. She was certain he'd been thinking of his own son when he'd felt her baby's movements. It had been written all over his face when he'd pulled away from her. She'd never meant to cause him pain, but it seemed as if that's all she ever did with Judah.

What had she been thinking? Why had she been so inconsiderate as to invite him to feel her baby kicking? She had gotten carried away in the joyful moment and she'd wanted to share it with someone. She was going to have to remind herself that they were no longer friends...or anything else for that matter.

The stunned look on Judah's face had been heart-breaking. And it had been a direct result of the little bundle growing inside of her. With an expressive face like Judah's, it was impossible to ignore his feelings.

If only she had kept her excitement to herself. The moment had come out of the blue, leaving her incredibly flustered. There hadn't been time for her to play it cool. The life growing inside her was a constant source of happiness.

Autumn placed her hands on her baby bump. A moment that had brought so much delight to her had left Judah reeling. Sometimes life was so complicated.

Running into Judah this afternoon had been pure coincidence. She had been pleasantly surprised by his sweet relationship with Ida and the way he seemed to experience genuine joy in their interaction. He'd shown her glimpses of the man she had once known. She hadn't allowed herself to acknowledge it for quite some time, but she'd missed him over the years. His presence in her life had always been strong and steady. As solid as the Rock of Gibraltar.

And now, she was torn between her goals here in Serenity Peak and checking on Judah to make sure he was all right. Was it even her place to do so? She highly doubted he would welcome it. Their past was full of moments where he'd been the one to lift her up when she'd fallen. It was hard to ignore that he was a man who seemed to be in pain. Didn't she owe it to him to try to help?

Keep your focus on the baby and your career, she reminded herself. Sean had tried to warn her earlier today about the complications of being near Judah, but she hadn't wanted to listen. For some reason she always thought with emotion when it came to her first love rather than common sense. Judah was a complication to all of her best-laid plans in Serenity Peak. She needed to remember why she had come back home in the first place and that it had absolutely nothing to do with Judah Campbell.

Chapter Seven

Autumn woke up to the aroma of freshly cooked bacon and eggs. There was no way she could go back to sleep with these tantalizing smells wafting through the house. Her nose and a grumbling stomach led her to the kitchen where Cecily had left her a note along with a covered plate of food.

Good morning. I thought you and the baby might like some pancakes, bacon and eggs. Love, Cici.

The last few days her sister had shocked her with her thoughtfulness. Flowers for no reason. A foot massage. A romance novel written by her favorite author. And now this scrumptious breakfast. It served as a reminder that she needed to try harder to foster a good relationship between them. She devoured her breakfast, finishing with a tall glass of orange juice. After hand washing her dishes and placing them on the rack, Autumn went into high gear.

It was time to get to work, she realized. This article wasn't going to write itself. Even though she had been a freelance journalist back in New York City, Autumn still felt a little rusty. She couldn't think of the last time she'd actually met someone in person to interview them for a piece. So much was done online or over the phone these days. Butterflies soared around in her stomach. She felt as nervous as a kid on the first day of school.

She dressed casually in a purple cashmere sweater and a pair of jeans. She could barely zip them up anymore thanks to her rounded belly. She'd purchased a bunch of maternity clothes, but she still hadn't worn any of them. Judging by the way these jeans were fitting, it was high time she did.

Thanks to Judah's list of contacts, she was making headway in setting up interviews. This morning she had arranged to meet two brothers—Brody and Caden Locke. Brody worked on the Fishful Thinking with Judah while Caden was a local pilot. Both had longstanding ties to the local fishing community. They also had generations of fishermen in their family. Since Serenity Peak was on the water and accessible only by air or ferry or boat, fishing had always been a huge industry.

Meeting at Northern Lights wasn't an option. The restaurant was popular and tended to get hectic at this time of day. She didn't want to have to talk loudly over the din of the crowd or be interrupted by acquaintances. Brody had suggested they meet at Humbled, a popular coffee shop on Fifth Street that had a connecting bookstore next door. Owned by Skye's best friend, Molly Truitt, it was a wonderful way to combine a love of books with an appreciation of coffee.

Autumn arrived early and ordered a green tea since she was steering clear of java during her pregnancy. There was a large selection of baked goods—scones, muffins, coffee cakes and an assortment of bagels.

"I highly recommend the lemon blueberry scone," Molly said, smiling at Autumn as she eyeballed the baked goods. "They're the perfect blend of tart and savory." With long brown hair that she wore in a single braid and round-shaped glasses, Molly always came across as more youthful than her actual age.

"I ate breakfast not too long ago, but I can't resist a good scone," Autumn said.

The ambiance of the coffee shop was warm and cozy. The walls were covered with Bible quotes and stunning pictures of Alaska. There were comfy love seats, plush couches and retro beanbags to sit on. The walls had been painted a calming eggshell color with little splashes of pink and baby blue. The vibe was soothing and peaceful, which was perfect for Autumn's mood. It was exactly what she needed in her life.

Autumn took her tea and the scone over to a comfy looking love seat. After sinking down into it she realized that she might have some trouble getting up. Her center of gravity was completely off-kilter these days. A few minutes later the brothers walked into the café. Although she vaguely remembered both from when she'd lived in Serenity Peak, they'd changed quite a bit since they were kids. They were fraternal twins, but to Autumn, they barely looked like members of the same family. Both were handsome men. Brody was just under six feet and more compact than Caden, who was tall with a rugged frame. The brothers had warm russet tones to their skin and kind brown eyes.

"You must be Autumn. I'm Brody. And this is my brother, Caden," Brody said by way of introduction. Both men reached out and shook Autumn's hand before sitting down on the couch next to her love seat.

"Thanks for coming. I really appreciate it," Autumn said. "Can I get you anything to drink or eat? It's the least I could do as a thank you for meeting up with me."

"No, thanks," Caden said. "I think we're all set."

"Judah said you're writing a piece about the fishing industry in the Kenai Peninsula," Brody said. "What in particular did you want to know?"

"I work for the *Alaska Tribune*. This is my first piece for them and it's an overview of the local fishing industry. As you know there's been a lot of ups and downs over the past few years with many fishermen suffering big financial losses."

Brody and Caden exchanged a glance. "Is this about the feds investigating?" Brody asked. "We've heard rumors but nothing specific to this area."

"To be honest, I haven't been able to get any information as to whether the authorities are close to charging anyone or if it's merely a rumor. As a result, I'm not going to lead with the alleged fraud," Autumn explained. "I'm going to wait for further developments."

"The authorities are keeping it close to the vest from what I've heard, which is why rumors are swirling around," Brody said. "There have been irregularities for years in the fishing industry, but all I know is that the fishermen I work with are above reproach. No one is altering the books or overfishing in off-limit areas."

"That's the frustrating thing," Caden said. "It's not right for a few dishonest fishermen to tarnish the entire profession."

"There have been whispers about Judah," Brody admitted. "None of it is true. I've worked alongside him for five years. He's as honest and hardworking as they come."

Brody was only confirming what Autumn already knew about Judah, although it was nice to know that his colleagues respected him.

"I'm curious though. What do you think is going on?" Autumn asked. Every instinct told her that the rumors about Judah were way off base. But who was behind them?

"There's someone who used to work for Judah. Scott Purdue. He was let go because he was caught cutting corners. He started his own operation, and so far, it's not doing too well," Brody explained. "I really think he's trying to trash Judah's reputation by starting a whisper campaign against him."

"Makes sense," she said, pausing to type notes on her iPad. It was a lot easier than jotting everything down in a notebook. She wasn't comfortable publishing anything about Purdue without tangible proof, but this information might help her in the future. "I haven't heard anything negative from my source about Judah. All of the whispers are coming from the local community, which is also unusual."

"My guess is it's coming from the same person. He's

smearing Judah's name because he's his competition," Caden added.

"Plus, he's angry about being let go. He's not the sort to forget," Brody said, his expression darkening. Both Caden and Brody were firmly in Judah's corner. Their loyalty was unbreakable.

And if there was one thing she knew for certain it was that Judah Campbell wasn't the type of man to commit fraud. He may have changed due to a family tragedy, but his core values remained intact. He came from a lineage of fishermen—proud, hardworking men who had carved out a living for themselves in a harsh and oftentimes unforgiving climate. As a journalist she had to remind herself to keep an open mind, but she believed in Judah's integrity.

For the next hour Autumn talked about the highs and lows of being a fisherman in Serenity Peak as well as their individual experiences. Although both men were overwhelmingly positive, neither one sugarcoated the drawbacks. Autumn found herself entertained by their comedic stories and equally moved by the struggles commercial fishermen faced. By the time the brothers headed out, Autumn felt like they were old friends. And she now had a bunch of ideas floating around in her head about how to tackle her subject matter. Fishermen were the heart and soul of the Kenai Peninsula. Instead of them being under the umbrella of suspicion, they should be lauded. Praised and respected. Her heart swelled at the idea of writing about such an honorable Alaskan profession.

She would continue to investigate fraud within the

local fishing community, in the hopes of exposing the guilty parties in the series finale. And if she uncovered some information to help Judah in the process, all the better.

The smell of the Bay rose to Judah's nostrils, salty and briny. It was such a part of him now, as constant as the sun that rose every day in the sky. He breathed in deeply as he watched a glaucous-winged gull swoop down low across the water. Judah raised his hand in greeting to a few of his crew members who had arrived and were heading on to the boat.

Judah had surprised himself by phoning Autumn the other day and throwing out some dates for her to accompany him on Fishful Thinking. He still wondered if it was the right call, but it was too late to backtrack now. Autumn was supposed to be meeting him here at the waterfront any minute now. He had already given his crew the heads up so that no one would be taken off guard by her appearance. It was usually just him and the crew. Since she was Sean's sister, Judah knew they would greet her with open arms.

The tomato red truck came barreling into the parking lot before pulling up a few feet away from him. Seconds later Autumn emerged from the truck carrying a small duffel bag. Dressed in an olive green thick parka and a pair of long rain boots, she had come prepared for a day at sea. A black beanie perched on her head completed the look. For the life of him, Judah couldn't ever remember someone looking so stunning for a day out on his boat.

"I hope I'm not late," she said, sounding out of breath. "I burned some toast this morning and set off all the alarms."

"You're right on time," Judah reassured her. "Are you sure about this? It gets rocky out there when the waves get rough."

"I'm very sure," she said. "I've never gotten seasick a day in my life. This isn't my first time on a commercial fishing boat."

But you weren't pregnant then, he wanted to say. He held his tongue. Autumn was grown enough to make her own decisions. He didn't want to come across as trying to dissuade her even though he worried about her being uncomfortable.

"Let's get started then," he said, walking toward the pier where Fishful Thinking was docked. Judah felt a burst of pride as they drew closer to the boat. To own his own fishing boat and employ a crew had been his dream ever since he was a kid. Autumn had been right alongside him as he'd dreamt big. And he had made them all come true.

"This is a great size," she said, just as he held out his hand for her to step from the dock onto the boat. He watched as she looked around. "It's beautiful," she said. "Your dad must have been really proud."

"He was," Judah acknowledged. Autumn had been one of his dad's favorite people. They had gotten along so well and fully understood one another. "He often said that he wished he was twenty years younger so he could be one of my crew members." The memory didn't sting like it normally did, but instead settled over him with the warmth of a cozy blanket. "All of this is because of him."

"Not all of it, Judah. It came to fruition because of your vision and hard work. Kurt would never want to take credit for your accomplishments."

Autumn was right. His father had been a humble and generous man who thankfully had lived to see Judah make a success out of his fishing outfit. Missing him was a part of his everyday life, but lately it was more of an ache than the sharp twist of a knife. He had been sick for a while and Judah had known the end was coming, which was a lot better than being blindsided by an accident.

"Just make sure to steer clear of the action," Judah advised. "I don't have a problem with you observing from a distance, but it's unsafe for you to be too close to the crew. You might get bumped by accident or get tangled up in something. Plus, I'm giving you a life jacket just in case something goes awry." He saw Autumn opening her mouth to protest. "It's the only way I can make this work so I'm not questioning my sanity. Agreed?"

Autumn's frown led him to believe she was going to fight him on the rules he'd laid out. He folded his arms across his chest and held her gaze as she stared him down. She let out a huff of air, then said, "Okay. Your boat. Your rules."

Every time he turned around, Autumn was there, watching him and his crew's every move like a hawk from a safe distance. She had a little notebook where she scribbled things down. Judah wasn't surprised when it got waterlogged and she had to abandon it. She seemed to take it in stride, shaking her head and smiling. He couldn't be sure, but Autumn seemed to be having fun.

"How are you doing?" Judah asked when he had a free moment to check on her. She was looking on as his crew netted herring and arctic char. There wasn't a single detail she didn't seem interested in. He could tell by her furrowed brow and the look of intense concentration etched on her face.

"This is great," she said. "Being here brings back a lot of memories."

Judah knew exactly what she meant. Back when they'd first started dating, Judah had invited her out on his father's boat—the Alaskan—on several occasions. For Judah it had been a test of sorts to see if she could handle the fisherman lifestyle. Autumn had passed with flying colors and managed to wrap the entire Campbell family around her little finger. She'd even landed the catch of the day, a King Salmon. Leif had crowned her Queen of the Bay. The nickname had stuck long after their excursion ended.

"Those were good times," he said. Judah surprised himself with the admission. He had been head over heels in love with Autumn back in the day. Everything between them had been near perfect, with talk of marriage and kids coming up from time to time between them. Then, without warning, Autumn had broken up with him with little or no explanation. He had been shattered and confused, but he'd been forced to accept her decision. Frankly, he wasn't sure he had ever gotten over it. On the rebound, he'd begun dating Mary and quickly dived into a serious relationship. Looking back on it, he had still been licking his wounds when things got started between him and Mary. There had been numerous times when she'd called him on it, but he'd blindly denied her assertions.

"Some of the best moments of my life," Autumn continued. "There's something so carefree about being out on the open water. I've really been looking forward to it. It's almost as if we're in our own world, isn't it? I can see why you love it so much." Her expressive features were lit up like rays of sunshine.

Autumn had always understood the lure of the water and why being a fisherman had been his life's passion. His dream job. He'd always believed that this meant they were made for one another. But he couldn't have been more wrong.

"My son loved being out here too." He let out a low chuckle. "Mary wasn't keen on boats. Believe it or not, she never learned to swim, but we gave Zane lessons at two years old. He swam like a minnow. He had the whole crew wrapped around his finger." His voice wobbled. "They called him Little Captain because he used to bark out orders like an adult."

"He sounds like a chip off the old block," Autumn said, grinning. "That must have made you proud."

"He was everything to me," Judah said in a muffled voice. He wasn't able to explain his son any better than that. Usually he avoided talking about him because when he did it felt as if he had shards of glass in his throat. Bringing up Zane had caused his soul to ache for all he'd lost in an instant. For whatever reason, the words had come today. He wondered if it was due to Autumn and their long history. And although the pain was still there, at least he could breathe normally. And chuckle. And remember Zane without wanting to smash something into pieces.

"I imagine he was…and will always be. Back in New York I had a friend who lost a child to cancer. I remember her saying that she would always be a mother and her child's life mattered. So she encouraged everyone to talk about her daughter and say her name. That way she wouldn't ever be forgotten."

Judah nodded. "Makes sense. Sometimes people don't want to mention Zane so as not to upset me. But it's way more painful to act like he wasn't here. To erase him like he never existed."

Autumn made a sympathetic sound. "That must be frustrating. I imagine most parents would want that affirmation."

He kept surprising himself by telling Autumn things he hadn't told a single soul. She had this effect on him unlike anyone else.

All of a sudden the water began churning violently with the boat rocking from side to side. A sudden groundswell caused Autumn to lose her footing and stumble on the slippery deck. Judah reached out and grabbed her parka, pulling her against him to prevent her from falling. He put his arms around her and anchored her to his chest as the boat continued to undulate. Autumn looked up at him with wide eyes. Her hands were on his chest for balance. He felt a little jolt at the contact. For a moment their gazes were locked as everything else around them faded away. She was standing so close to him Judah could see the little caramel flecks in her eyes and the small gold studs in her ears.

"Are you all right?" Judah asked, still holding her tightly. The idea of letting go of her left him with an empty feeling.

"I—I'm fine," she said. "I just lost my balance for a moment."

"I tried to warn you that the waters get choppy out here." Thoughts of her getting hurt wouldn't stop whirling around his mind. As the boat's captain it was his responsibility to safeguard everyone on board. He didn't want anything to happen to Autumn or the baby, especially not on his watch. And definitely not on his boat.

After making sure the vessel was no longer lurching, Judah let go of her.

"I know, Judah, but I wasn't in any danger," Autumn said. "Please don't worry about me. I'm a big girl."

Despite the chill in the air, a warm sensation spread through his chest. "True, but I'll always want to keep you safe, Autumn. Old habits die hard."

And that was the problem. After all this time and the years that stood between them, Judah still cared about Autumn way more than he wanted to. It was the main reason why being near her wasn't in his best interest. The last time around it had taken a long time to mend his shattered heart. There was no telling what could happen if he opened the door even a crack and let Autumn in. This time he might never recover.

Old habits die hard. That pretty much summed things up. Here she stood on the deck of Fishful Think-

ing filled with admiration for Judah. Watching him reel
in arctic char, haddock and herring had been an eye-
opener about what it took to operate a commercial fishing vessel. Under Judah's direction his crew was a finely
oiled machine. The camaraderie they shared was evident in the way they worked so well as a team. Seeing
their haul up close served as a reminder that the work
of Judah and his crew fed people and supported the seafood industry in Alaska.

Now she knew how Judah had kept his rugged frame
in such great shape all these years. There was a lot of
physicality in his job, and he was in constant motion
when he wasn't driving the vessel. Years ago when she
had gone out on the Alaskan with Judah's dad there
hadn't been much work involved since it was a pleasure trip, so she hadn't really known how everything
operated. By the time they docked back at harbor, Autumn felt as if she'd attended a master class in commercial fishing.

The experience of being out on Kachemak Bay so far
from land had been a thrilling adventure, far removed
from her daily life. With the wind whipping through
her hair and the heady scent of the Bay filling her nostrils, Autumn had been euphoric. Certain situations in
life made a person feel as if they were living life to the
fullest. This had been one of them. And that moment
where Judah had held her in order to prevent her from
stumbling had been heavily charged with electricity.
She now knew with a deep certainty that she hadn't
been imagining anything at Ida's house.

After they arrived back at the harbor, Autumn said

her goodbyes to the crew before making a beeline to Judah.

"I really appreciate you allowing me to go out on Fishful Thinking with you and the crew," Autumn said. She had chosen her words wisely. Today had been a gift—of his time and expertise, as well as Fishful Thinking and the crew. There had been such a strong sense of pride in their work that radiated from all of them. She couldn't remember ever feeling so impressed by a group of people.

Judah nodded. "I hope it helps with your article."

"More than you realize. I have a newfound admiration for your profession."

Judah nodded. "That's nice to hear. I'll pass it along to the crew." He jerked his chin in the direction of his crew members. "I've got to finish up before I have a mutiny. Take it easy, Autumn."

As she walked toward her truck, fatigue swept over her. She'd done a full day on Judah's boat, and she was beat and hungry. The lunch cooked by the crew on board had been hearty, but she was extra hungry these days as she entered her third trimester. Pretty soon she would be bringing a child into the world, something she hadn't thought possible.

Now that she had gone out on Fishful Thinking with Judah, she really wouldn't have much of a reason to be in contact with him. Along with the interviews she'd been doing, she would now have enough to flesh out an article. She should feel relieved, yet a part of her was lamenting the end of something. It was difficult to put her finger on her emotions, but she thought it might be tied up in the friendship they'd once shared. She missed sharing secrets and finishing each other's sentences. Nothing was as it used to be, but that didn't stop her wanting to see Judah whole again and healed.

Frankly, she didn't know if it was possible. She had always believed that with God anything was possible, but she wasn't even sure if Judah was a man of faith anymore. If she had to guess she would say he wasn't. Loss had rocked his world and shaken his faith, she imagined.

Perhaps it was for the best that she and Judah kept away from one another, she reasoned. Judah made her think of things she hadn't thought of in over a decade. And he made her feel guilty about the secret that had ended their relationship. Back in New York it had been easy to cast her lie of omission to the side and pretend as if it had never happened. But now that she was back in Serenity Peak and close to Judah, the lie was weighing heavily on her every time she gazed into his soulful blue eyes.

Chapter Eight

A loud knock sounded on Judah's front door, causing Delilah to let out a loud bark in response. The door swung open and his nephew, Ryan, strode into the house. With a head of dark hair and sky blue eyes, Ryan turned heads. He had a reputation in Serenity Peak as a charmer. In the past, it had gotten him in a bit of trouble. Ryan was a deputy in town, and he'd spent the last year trying to rework his image. All Judah saw when he looked at him was a good-hearted young man who at twenty-seven years old was still learning and growing.

"Hey, Unc. I heard you weren't out on Fishful Thinking today." Ryan headed straight toward where Judah was reclining in his living room. Delilah trailed behind Ryan, looking up at him as if he owed her a doggy treat.

Judah let out a groan. Gossip spread as fast as tornado winds in small towns. He hated being talked about. "How did you hear about it?" Two days ago he'd aggravated an old shoulder injury and he was taking a few days off due to the throbbing pain.

Get up to 4
FREE FABULOUS BOOKS
in your welcome box!

To thank you for being a loyal reader we'd like to send you up to 4 FREE BOOKS, absolutely free when you try the Harlequin Reader Service.

Just write "YES" on the Loyal Reader Voucher and we'll send you your welcome box with 2 free books from each series you choose plus free mystery gifts! Each welcome box is worth over $20.

Try **Love Inspired® Romance Larger-Print** and get 2 books and fall in love with inspirational romances that take you on an uplifting journey of faith, forgiveness and hope.

Try **Love Inspired® Suspense Larger-Print** and get 2 books where courage and optimism unite in stories of faith and love in the face of danger.

Or **TRY BOTH** and get 2 books from each series!

Your welcome box is completely free, even the shipping! If you continue with your subscription, you can look forward to curated monthly shipments of brand-new books from your selected series, always at a discount off the cover price! Plus you can cancel any time.

So don't miss out, return your Loyal Readers Voucher today to get your Free Welcome Box.

Pam Powers

LOYAL READER
FREE BOOKS VOUCHER
WELCOME BOX

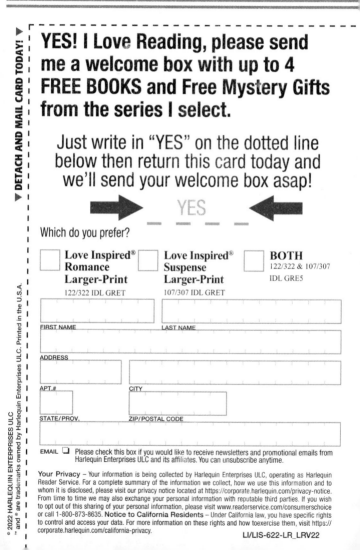

◀ **DETACH AND MAIL CARD TODAY!** ▼

YES! I Love Reading, please send me a welcome box with up to 4 FREE BOOKS and Free Mystery Gifts from the series I select.

Just write in "YES" on the dotted line below then return this card today and we'll send your welcome box asap!

➡ YES ⬅

Which do you prefer?

☐ **Love Inspired® Romance Larger-Print**
122/322 IDL GRET

☐ **Love Inspired® Suspense Larger-Print**
107/307 IDL GRET

☐ **BOTH**
122/322 & 107/307
IDL GRE5

FIRST NAME

LAST NAME

ADDRESS

APT.#

CITY

STATE/PROV.

ZIP/POSTAL CODE

EMAIL ☐ Please check this box if you would like to receive newsletters and promotional emails from Harlequin Enterprises ULC and its affiliates. You can unsubscribe anytime.

LI/LIS-622-LR_LRV22

"I ran into Brody, and he told me you were taking off a few days. It wasn't hard to figure out that you must be out of commission, because you never miss a day of work." Ryan's tone was matter-of-fact. He held up a paper bag. "I brought some reinforcements." The smell of savory meat and grilled food rose to his nostrils. How mad could he be since Ryan had brought food along with him?

Judah winced as he tried to sit up on his couch. "It's my shoulder. I think that I pulled a muscle. I just need to rest it for a few days and use some heating pads and take pain relievers." He didn't bother to tell his nephew that he had been getting cortisone injections in his shoulder for the past few years.

"Let me know if you need any Bengay," Ryan said, bursting into laughter despite his best attempt to keep a straight face. His nephew enjoyed acting as if Judah was as old as Methuselah. He couldn't count the number of times he'd made this joke.

Judah frowned. "Ha ha. You're hilarious."

Ryan placed the bag down on his coffee table and began taking out the food and making plates for both of them. He slid a plate over to Judah along with utensils and a water.

"So I heard Autumn went out on the boat with you a few days ago." Ryan flashed a broad smile. He was the spitting image of Leif when he was in his midtwenties.

Judah let out a groan. "Brody has a big mouth," Judah said.

"I never said it was Brody," Ryan said with a chuckle. "Did you throw your back out showing off for her?"

Judah glared at him. "Did you just come over here to aggravate me?"

"Pretty much. Is she still as gorgeous as ever?" Ryan asked.

"Even more so if that's possible," Judah admitted. "She's writing an article on the fishing community so I did her a favor. End of story."

Ryan had a wistful expression etched on his face. "I had the biggest crush on her when I was a kid."

Both Judah and Autumn had been well aware of his nephew's affection for Autumn. She had viewed his fondness as sweet and heartwarming.

"She's having a baby in a few months."

Ryan drew his dark brows together. "Whoa. I didn't see that plot twist coming."

Neither did I, Judah wanted to say. He bit his tongue, knowing if he did it would only add flames to the fire. He wondered if anyone was whispering about him and Autumn. Not that there was anything going on, but everyone in town knew their history and the gossip mill already knew she'd been out on his boat.

Judah quickly filled him in on her marital status. "She wants to raise her baby here. By herself. Sounds like her ex is completely out of the picture."

Ryan let out a low whistle as he dished out the food on to Styrofoam plates. He settled down into a seat across from Judah. "That's admirable. Raising a baby as a single mother won't be easy. She's going to face a lot of challenges."

"If anyone can rise to the occasion it's Autumn," Judah said forcefully.

Ryan raised a brow. "So, is there any chance the two of you can find your way back to one another? A reunion romance?"

"No!" he said sharply. "That's all water under the bridge. We ended things a long time ago. Or should I say she was the one who kicked me to the curb." Back then his pride had prevented him from fighting back and questioning her decision. He had been so hurt and wounded by her decision to end things between them. Why hadn't he pressed her for a reason? Even to this day, her decision hadn't made much sense. She'd loved him. Of that he was certain.

"Ouch," Ryan said, quirking his mouth. "I didn't know that."

"It's ancient history," Judah said with a shrug. No matter how many times he tried to convince himself of that fact it still rang hollow. Seeing her again after all these years had brought their relationship back to the forefront.

"Okay, so will you be making an appearance at the festival?" Ryan asked before putting a forkful of food in his mouth.

Serenity Peak would be hosting its annual Midnight Sun festival featuring live music, art, vendors, food trucks and dancing. It had always been the town's ultimate event. The past few years he hadn't attended the celebration. This year would be no different. The last thing he wanted to do was schmooze with people he couldn't trust.

"Probably not," Judah said bluntly. Being at town events wasn't his thing. He hated the idea of being whispered about and gawked at like he was a character in a sideshow. He didn't feel comfortable being at the center of things. Before the accident he'd loved any and all opportunities to mix and mingle with the townsfolk. But all that had changed in an instant.

"I was hoping it would give you and my dad an opportunity to talk. This impasse between the two of you has gone on too long." Ryan heaved a big sigh. "As you well know, tomorrow isn't promised."

"Ryan, I know you're coming from a good place, but I have my reasons to keep a distance from Leif." His brother had continued to do business with some of the folks who had spread ugly whispers about Mary after the crash. His brother had chosen business and a paycheck over Judah and his family. Although Leif had tried on several occasions to repair their relationship, Judah hadn't been interested. Some fissures couldn't ever be mended. There was still an ache in his chest knowing their estrangement couldn't be mended.

Ryan quirked his mouth. "We miss them too, you know. Zane was my little buddy. Dad loved him just as much as you love me. I know your whole life was rocked to the core when you lost them, but you're still alive. You still have people who love you."

His nephew's words were humbling. Sometimes he did tend to forget that he wasn't the only one who had suffered a tremendous loss. Ryan and Zane had been incredibly close. The very night of the accident Ryan had taken Zane out for pizza before dropping him back home. Hours later he was gone.

"I really appreciate you sharing that with me," Judah

said. "It means a lot. And in case I've never told you, I want to thank you for being such a good role model for Zane. You were like a big brother to him."

Ryan's eyes looked moist, and he forcefully cleared his throat. "I'll never forget him. I just want to make sure you're in a place where you can move forward. Aunt Mary would want that for you. So would Zane."

He knew his wife and son would want healing for him. But at some point he needed to want it for himself.

"I'm doing the best I can, Ry. I really am." Maybe his actions didn't look like much from the outside, but every day he'd been fighting his way through grief. For the first few years it had seemed as if he was walking through quicksand. Only in the last year had Judah begun to find his way out of the darkness. And even now he still had moments where he struggled to make sense of such a devastating loss. He had crawled through glass to get to where he was today.

"Do you need anything before I head out?" Ryan asked. "You might benefit from a hot shower."

"Can you get me one of those medicated patches on the kitchen counter?" Judah asked. He wasn't due for another cortisone shot for a few weeks and the patches helped him get through an episode.

"Sure thing," Ryan said, grabbing their plates and the bag before heading toward the kitchen. A few minutes later he returned with the patches and handed them over to Judah.

"Nice catching up, Unc," Ryan said as he headed toward the door. "I'd love to see you at the festival… so would Dad."

"But you won't," Judah said after the door closed. He wished that he could simply say yes and make an appearance at the festival, but he couldn't face a town that had turned its back on him when he'd needed them the most.

The following day, Autumn was at Northern Lights helping Sean out with his inventory. The work wasn't difficult, but she found it incredibly monotonous. After hours of standing, she headed into her brother's office to put her feet up and have a snack. Autumn had found that if she didn't eat something every few hours her energy levels began to dip. So far pregnancy had been kind to her, but she'd begun to notice fatigue throughout the day. She had made an effort to stay hydrated and active to combat her symptoms as Doc Poppy had advised.

A sudden noise caused her to swing her gaze up. Judah stood in the doorway dressed casually in a pair of dark jeans and a hunter green colored sweater. She was surprised to see him here, knowing he was usually on his boat in the early afternoon.

"Hey there. I was looking for Sean. Is he playing hooky today?" Judah asked.

Autumn smiled. "Hi, Judah. He actually had some errands to run with Helene so I'm covering for him." Helene was Sean's wife of almost twenty years. They had gotten married when they were barely twenty-one. Autumn liked to say they were still as giddy about each other as they'd been in high school. It made Autumn continue to believe that loving relationships were possible if both people put in the work and honored their commitment.

Judah gave her propped up feet a pointed look.

"I've been working really hard all day. I only stopped a few minutes ago."

"Working hard or hardly working?" he asked. The corners of his mouth twitched with laughter.

Autumn put her feet back on solid ground. "Seriously?"

"I was teasing you," he said. "Please put your feet back up and relax. You deserve it."

This, she thought, was the old rapport they had once shared with Judah always joking and laughing. The push and pull of their friendship had led to romance.

"Was that you I saw leaving the clinic this morning?" she asked. "Either that or you have an identical twin." She had beeped as she'd driven past, but Judah hadn't looked in her direction.

Earlier this morning she'd had her prenatal appointment with Doc Poppy. On her way into the parking lot she had gotten a glimpse of Judah driving away.

"Yeah, it was me. I've been off work for a few days due to my shoulder acting up. My doctor took pity on me and gave me a cortisone shot a few weeks early." He rotated his shoulder. "It already feels much better. I've been doing everything at home to make it feel better."

Autumn made a face. "Sounds painful. I'm glad they could help you out."

She hadn't seen Judah since the day on his boat. Autumn still felt grateful for his assistance in allowing her to observe operations on Fishful Thinking. Maybe they could be friends after all. Perhaps she had been overthinking things. Or was influenced by the guilt she felt for holding on to the secret from their shared past. No matter how she tried to bury it, she couldn't ignore the fact that she'd ended their relationship rather than tell him about being infertile. She had broken up with him under false pretenses, which was tantamount to a lie.

"So, how are the articles coming?" he asked as he stepped closer toward the desk.

"I have some holes to fill in, but they're coming along nicely. A few more weeks and I should be done with the entire series. The first article will come out next week." Once the fishing series was finished, Autumn would write a few articles about coming home to Alaska and a feature on dog musher Ace Reynolds, before taking some time off to welcome the baby and enjoy maternity leave.

"That's great. Sounds like you've made a lot of progress after the interviews." Judah seemed pleased for her which left her feeling encouraged.

"Talking to people who have ties to the fishing community made all the difference." She nibbled on her lip. "When I did the interviews some information came up about your name being tied to the fraud investigation."

Judah bristled. "I really don't want to get into all of that. I do my best to just focus on my work and not get dragged into the muck."

"Why not? If someone's trying to tarnish your reputation don't you want to know who it is?" she pressed.

"Not really," he said with a shrug. "I know I'm honest and hardworking. Furthermore, not a single official has contacted me about this investigation, which lets me know that I'm not under the microscope. As long as no one's trying to take away my business I'm good."

She let out a ragged breath. "That's funny because when you first found out I was writing a piece for the *Tribune* you seemed mighty concerned that I might be targeting you."

"And you assured me you weren't. End of story," he spit out. "Or so I thought," he muttered. "Now it seems as if you're just poking and prying into stuff that's none of your concern."

She stood up and threw her hands up in the air. "I just don't get it. Everyone I talked to wants to defend you and here you are acting blasé about everything."

"Leave it alone. I never asked for help. I don't need it. I'm good."

Autumn let out a snort. "Of course you didn't because you're enjoying being Judah against the world. You don't need anyone, right? How's that working out for you?" She folded her arms across her middle. At this point they were mere inches from one another. Both of them were speaking in raised voices. The tension between them was palpable. It crackled in the air between them.

Judah took a step closer toward her so there were only a few inches resting between them. A vein pulsed alongside his jaw and his breathing sounded uneven. "Autumn, you actually have no idea what's going on with me. None! You swept back into town after a twelve-year absence acting like a know-it-all. Trust me, you don't know half as much as you think you do about anything in Serenity Peak, never mind the fishing industry." His nostrils flared and he was breathing heavily. "You see, that's what happens when you're missing in action for over a decade." He curled his lip. "I don't have time for this, especially not today."

Judah stormed away from her, his strides full of anger. Seconds later she heard the back door slam shut with a thunderous bang.

Her whole body was trembling from their encounter. How had things gotten so out of control within seconds? Everything had spiraled downward in an instant. Judah was like a powder keg.

Just then Cecily raced into Sean's office. Her eyes were wide as she looked at Autumn. "Are you all right? I heard shouting."

"Yes, I'm fine," she said in a quivering voice, "but Judah isn't. He stormed out of here like a tornado." She ran a shaky hand through her hair. *What in the world had set him off? Didn't he realize that she'd been trying to help him?*

At this point she was ready to throw in the towel and stop trying to establish any kind of friendship between them. Why was she trying so hard anyway when Judah clearly wanted a life of isolation? It was almost as if he always picked a fight with her to deliberately alienate her.

"Hey, it's not you," Cecily said, placing her arm around Autumn. "Really, it isn't."

Autumn scoffed. "I think you're wrong about that, sis. Every time I think Judah's turning a corner, he shows me he's a wounded bear with a thorn in his paw. And I'm always the one to set him off." She wasn't going to admit it to her sister, but it really hurt her feelings to have him lash out at her. She ached to get to a place where they were on an even keel, but at some point Autumn needed to let it go.

"I'm not excusing his behavior, but he has every reason to be upset today." Cecily bit her lip. "It's Zane's birthday. He would have been eleven years old today."

Autumn shut her eyes and let out a groan. "Oh, how awful. I had no idea." Of course she didn't. As Judah had made clear, Autumn had been MIA from Serenity Peak for a long time. She was just now getting acclimated and playing catch-up on everything she had missed. There was no way she could have known, but if she had, Autumn would have kept their conversation light and easy.

"Judah was probably already having an awful day when I went and upset him. I can't imagine what's going through his mind." Why hadn't she kept her mouth shut? In trying to help Judah she'd poked the bear and riled him up.

"I'm guessing it didn't take much to unravel him on a day like this," Cecily said.

"I wish there was something we could do to ease the pain for him," Autumn said. Her heart felt heavy for Judah. No matter their differences, she still cared about him. Even if he didn't want her to, she would continue to do so. Most likely from a distance.

"I know, Autumn, but I don't think Judah is in a place right now to accept any help. He's intent on dealing with all of this pain by himself." Her sister shrugged. "He's been pushing everyone away for years. Some days I really think I'm seeing glimpses of the old Judah, but it never lasts for long."

Cecily was right! Judah didn't want help or a shoulder to lean on. He wanted to be alone to grapple with his emotions. Maybe he needed to honor this day by himself. Perhaps it should be a day of reflection. She prayed that his memories of Zane would sustain him, not only for today but for all the days to follow.

Lord, please hold Judah in the palm of your hand. Protect him. Nurture him. And guide him until he comes back to You.

Chapter Nine

There weren't many places where Judah could go in Serenity Peak that brought him absolute peace. The Halcyon Mountains were a rare exception. Beautiful and majestic, the peaks boasted the most breathtaking views he had ever seen in his life. If he stood on a certain ridge, Judah could see all of Serenity Peak, as well as Kachemak Bay. Ever since he was a kid, Judah had been hiking these trails and exploring the mountain's hidden gems. The air up here was pristine, and the clouds seemed to be within reach.

"I thought that I might find you here." Sean's voice came from behind him.

Judah had been so deep in his thoughts that he hadn't heard his best friend approaching. Even though Judah often gave off standoffish vibes, Sean knew better. He understood instinctively that Judah didn't want to be alone today. There was something about this eleventh birthday remembrance that was hitting him particularly hard. Maybe it was because turning eleven had been full of such joy and wonder for Judah. If anyone were to have asked him he would have told them it was his favorite birthday year.

"He loved being up here in the mountains. I wanted to spend some time in a place he adored." Judah shoved his hands into his parka pockets. "I've never seen him quite so happy as when we came out here."

"I get it," Sean said. "It's a nice way to honor him. He was an amazing kid, Judah. Someone special that's for sure. He had a light and a raw energy that dazzled all of us."

"Did you know he could recognize ten different species of birds by the time he was six?" Judah let out a chuckle. "That used to make Mary so proud. Not that it took much. She was his biggest fan."

Silence settled in as they looked out over the valley. Time seemed to stand still here. That quality was comforting to him. He didn't have to worry about everything whirling and speeding past him.

"I blew up at Autumn earlier. I'm feeling pretty torn up about it." Ever since he'd left Northern Lights he had been filled with recriminations. Things had gotten so ugly between them. Even though he'd been annoyed with Autumn poking around in his business, he'd been in a bad way ever since he had woken up. She didn't deserve to be a scapegoat.

The fact that he should be celebrating Zane's eleventh birthday today instead of mourning him caused his soul to ache. It wasn't fair! *Why Zane, God? Why did you pick my son?* The question had been reverberating inside his mind ever since the accident.

"I know. She told me." Sean shook his head. "The two of you have unfinished business, Judah. Maybe you should just hash out the past with her so you can move forward…as friends…acquaintances. Whatever you decide."

"Hash what out? She dumped me. What's there to talk about?" he asked.

Sean shrugged. "I don't know, man. There was always something odd about the breakup if you ask me. She was so into you. And now there just feels like something is fueling this discord between you."

Judah soaked in Sean's words. They made a lot of sense. He had always known there had been words left unspoken between him and Autumn. Pride was a powerful emotion. He'd been so gutted by the breakup he hadn't stuck around to ask any questions. Judah had retreated into his own solitude in order to lick his wounds. Some things never changed. He'd done the same thing after the accident. And what had it gotten him? A whole lot of nothing.

As they walked back down the trail to the bottom, Sean turned to him. "I have something for you." He held up his hands and said, "It's a little bit cheesy, but also really meaningful."

"Okay," Judah said. He had no idea what Sean was talking about, but he had a feeling he was about to find out.

When they got closer to where their vehicles were parked, Judah immediately noticed balloons peeking through the half-lowered windows of Sean's truck.

"Balloons? You bought me balloons?" Judah asked. He looked at Sean and raised an eyebrow.

"Yes," Sean said with a nod. "Eleven balloons to be precise. To celebrate how old he would be today. We can release them into the sky as a remembrance of Zane."

Sean shifted from one foot to the other. "If that's okay with you."

For a moment Judah couldn't respond. He wasn't sure he could get any words out. His throat felt clogged with emotion.

"Or I can just take them back home with me," Sean said. He was suddenly looking sheepish as if he might have made a wrong move.

"No, don't do that," Judah said. "Zane loved balloons. He couldn't get enough of them." Judah chuckled at a memory of his son filling up water balloons on the first day of summer and bombarding his parents with them. This would be the perfect low-key way to celebrate his birthday.

Sean grinned and reached through the window to collect the strings. Judah stepped forward to assist him as he opened the truck's door. Judah stood with Sean as they released each blue balloon into the air, one by one. When they were done, Judah watched as Sean lowered his head and crossed his hands in front of him. More than anything, Judah wanted to follow suit and pray for his son, but the words wouldn't come. It was frustrating, but he couldn't force things.

His heart was lighter now. "Thanks for putting this together," he said, clapping Sean on the shoulder. "It's not something that I would have ever thought of doing, but it was perfect."

"I can't take the credit for it though. This was all Autumn. It was her idea, Judah. She didn't know Zane, but she wanted to help you celebrate him."

Judah sucked in a shocked breath. *Autumn! Sweet, thoughtful Autumn.* The fact that she had come up with this way to honor his son was touching. Especially after the way he'd lashed out at her earlier. But that was Autumn's nature. She had never harbored grudges and always worked hard at forgiveness. He could learn a lot from the way she lived her life, he realized.

For so long now he had been harboring resentments against all of the townsfolk. Deep down he had always known it was unfair to blame an entire town for the actions of a few. But doing so had served a purpose at the time, allowing him to retreat into his own surroundings so he could mourn and rage against the unfairness of the bottom falling out of his world.

Autumn extending him grace was an eye-opener. It had him thinking about his own actions and what kind of man he wanted to be. His father's favorite passage came to mind. *And be ye kind one to another, tenderhearted, forgiving one another, even as God for Christ's sake hath forgiven you.* Judah wasn't living up to any of those principles.

For so long now everyone in his life had been stepping up for him. It was high time he took some steps of his own toward healing.

Chapter Ten

Serenity Peak's downtown area was bursting with excitement as crowds gathered to celebrate the Midnight Sun festival. Delicious aromas wafted in the air as people lined up to order from the food trucks and other vendors. Autumn grinned at the shaved ice truck parked by the town green. That was a new one in Alaska. Tents had been set up for pie-eating contests and jewelry making. She tapped her foot to the beat of a band performing live music as townsfolk took to a makeshift dance floor. Everywhere around her there were smiling faces and residents enjoying themselves. She ran into former classmates and a few of her former teachers. It felt really nice to be welcomed back to town with such enthusiasm.

Getting ready for the event had made Autumn feel like a younger version of herself. Every year her family had attended the festival together as a unit. They had made incredible memories that were now indelibly imprinted on her heart. Someday soon her child would be attending and having just as much fun. Yet another moment she could look forward to in her future.

The festival was an all-day affair, going from mid-morning to midnight. Although Autumn knew she wouldn't stay until midnight, she was looking forward to being here and celebrating with the townsfolk.

She made her way over to the table hosted by Northern Lights. Sean, Cecily and her sister-in-law, Helene, were standing there handing out desserts. Sean had decided not to sell any food today. Instead, he was giving away desserts for free. The offer was good for as long as the scrumptious treats lasted. Autumn shook her head at the massive line.

"Your sweets are in high demand," Autumn said as she made her way to the table.

"Tell me about it," Sean said, wiping his brow with his forearm. "We're going to run out soon at this rate."

"*My* confections, thank you very much," Cecily said proudly. "Key lime tarts. Wild berry cobbler. Coconut cream puffs. And that's just a sampling." She was practically puffing out her chest. Her sister had been making all of the desserts for the restaurant for the last six months. Sales had almost doubled according to the books.

"You really need to get a side gig going, Cici," Autumn said. "You'd make a small fortune."

"Don't encourage her," Sean said. "Her desserts are the reason sales are up."

"Desserts by Cecily," her sister said. "I can totally see it."

Sean let out a groan as the sisters and Helene laughed. They all knew Cecily wasn't going anywhere although

Autumn thought Sean should offer her sister the opportunity to buy a stake in the business.

This was nice. She hadn't hung out with her siblings in a very long time. This was overdue and it reminded her of all the good times from their childhood. It was comforting knowing she could look forward to more moments of togetherness in the years to come.

"As I live and breathe. Look who's here," Cecily said in a raised voice. Autumn followed Cecily's gaze. Judah! He was walking straight toward them with a look of uncertainty plastered on his face.

Her pulse began to quicken at the sight of him. In a million years she'd never expected Judah to show up at a town event. He had made it quite clear that he wasn't interested in being part of the fabric of Serenity Peak.

"Hey, everyone. How's it going?" Judah asked. "It's a beautiful day for a festival."

Sean and Cecily greeted him warmly as Autumn stepped to the side and focused on handing out desserts. After their argument the other day, she didn't know how to speak to him with such awkwardness sitting between them.

A few moments later Judah walked up beside her. With stubble on his chin, he looked rugged and way too handsome for his own good. After all this time she still felt a little jolt when she laid eyes on him.

"Autumn," Judah said. "Can we talk for a moment?" His blue eyes threatened to bore a hole straight through her. She always found it hard to look away when he gazed into her eyes.

"Sure," she said, bracing for more awkwardness. She walked a few steps away from the table so they could speak privately. "What's up?" she asked, trying to sound casual.

"I want to apologize for the other day," Judah said. "It wasn't right for me to raise my voice at you or say the things I did." Their gazes locked and Autumn saw the sincerity radiating from his eyes. "Zane's birthday always hits me hard. But that's no excuse for lighting into you."

She ran her hand through her hair, nervously winding a few strands around her fingers. "I can't imagine how painful the birthdays are for you. It's an unfathomable loss."

His intense gaze swept over her. "Sean told me the balloons were your idea. I don't have the words to tell you what that meant to me." His jaw trembled. "I've had such a difficult time trying to mark birthdays and anniversaries, so your gesture was spot-on. I don't think I'll ever forget it."

A warm sensation spread through her chest upon hearing that the balloons had meant something to him. She had been at a loss as to how to help him navigate the day until the idea came to mind.

"I know you've had a rough time of it, Judah. And that breaks my heart for you." She blinked away tears. "Of course I forgive you. Anyone can have a bad moment."

"I appreciate you being so gracious." He reached out for her hand and squeezed it. Autumn felt a little funny at the way their hands were joined. She was having a hard time ignoring the way his hand made her palm tingle with awareness. And it felt so solid in hers.

"I'm really happy you decided to come today, and I know so many folks who will be thrilled to see you."

Judah made a face. "Let's not get carried away," he said with a chuckle. "I'm just putting my baby toe in the water. I'm not sure that I actually want to talk to anyone. I don't want to lose my reputation as a man of mystery."

Autumn laughed along with him. "It's too late to turn back now."

Being able to laugh with Judah was heartwarming. Although his mood shifts were confusing, she now realized that he was still walking through his grieving process. He was a strong person to have made it through such a terrible loss without completely falling apart. The only real grief Autumn had ever known was related to her infertility diagnosis and the dissolution of her marriage. Being told she would never conceive a child had been devastating. She had been sad about the divorce, but certain that brighter days were ahead of her. She hoped Judah had things to look forward to in his future so that he could see tomorrow's promise.

"And it's a wrap," Sean called out. "All the desserts are gone."

Cecily and Autumn let out cheers at a job well done while some folks standing in line began to groan with disappointment.

"Always leave them wanting more," Helene said with a grin.

Judah jumped in to help Sean take down the table while Autumn grabbed the Northern Lights sign advertising free desserts. She didn't want anyone to see the poster and think that treats were still available.

As Sean and Helene headed out to locate their kids, Cecily took off to meet up with a few friends which left Autumn and Judah on their own. She was surprised when Judah asked her if she wanted to explore the event together. Autumn wasn't going to say no to Judah's invitation. She was really proud of him for showing up today. Although he didn't seem completely at ease being in this public setting, attending the event was a huge step in the right direction.

"So, I'm curious, what brought you to the festival?" Autumn asked Judah.

"I figured it was time. This is a step in moving forward. It's something I thought a lot about on Zane's birthday. Am I still angry that some folks in town tried to smear my wife's name? Yes, that won't ever sit well with me. But I love this town. I'm not going to let anyone take that away from me. I've been on the sidelines for too long now." He lifted his shoulders. "It's hard to explain, but something about Zane's birthday caused a shift inside of me."

"I couldn't agree more. You have so much to offer this town."

"Oh, really." Judah's eyes twinkled. "Tell me more. I'm listening." He cupped his hand to his ear.

Autumn felt her cheeks getting flushed. Judah's playful side was coming out and it was causing her stomach to do flip-flops. She didn't want him to think she'd been gushing about him. Autumn swatted at him and said, "I see you still have an overgrown ego. I was just being nice."

"Ouch," Judah said, placing his hand over his heart. "That hurts."

"In all seriousness, Serenity Peak needs you. You're honest and hardworking. You have so much integrity and deep ties to this community. That means something."

"Maybe I should run for mayor," Judah said. The sides of his mouth were twitching just before he broke out into a full-fledged smile.

"Stranger things have happened. What would your campaign slogan be?" she asked.

"Judah Campbell. Fishing for votes," he quipped. They both burst out laughing with neither one letting up. Autumn knew that they were drawing their fair share of curious looks, but she didn't care. For today she was going to put aside all the many reasons why she should steer clear of Judah. She was going to live in the moment and enjoy herself.

"I'd vote for you," she said, flashing him a grin. A look passed between them and all of a sudden the moment was full of a heightened energy that pulsed in the air.

"You two look like you're having way too much fun." Violet, accompanied by her son, Chase, sauntered up to them. Chase held a huge piece of fried dough smothered in cinnamon sugar in his hands. The mere sight of the sweet treat made Autumn's mouth water.

"It's great to see you, buddy," Judah said, reaching down and putting his hand on Chase's shoulder.

"You too," Chase said, looking up at him with a shy smile. "I missed you."

Autumn thought her heart might melt as Chase placed his little arms around Judah.

"I missed you too," Judah said as he hugged Chase back. "You've gotten so big I barely recognize you."

"I've been eating my vegetables. Even spinach," Chase said somberly as the adults laughed.

"We're headed over to the art tent," Violet said. "Picasso here wants to make a sand art masterpiece. We'll probably run into you later on."

"Have fun," Autumn said, waving.

"Call me," Violet said, wagging her eyebrows at Autumn behind Judah's back.

Autumn knew Violet was no doubt imagining all sorts of things about her and Judah, none of which were true. They were really just two people who were taking delicate steps at reestablishing a friendship. If she occasionally experienced belly flips or goosebumps in his presence it was simply due to their fractured past.

"Do you still like fried dough?" Judah asked. "I remember how you used to love it."

"Are you kidding me? It took every ounce of self-control I have not to snatch it from Chase and inhale it." She shook her head. "These pregnancy cravings are no joke. The other night I wanted peanut butter and marshmallows." She chuckled. "And I don't even like marshmallows."

"I say we go in search of fried dough. My treat," Judah offered. "You can even get seconds."

"How can I say no to that?" Autumn asked. She was thoroughly enjoying herself with Judah. So many memories of their shared past were coming back to her.

How many times had they enjoyed this very festival as a couple? They had walked hand in hand, danced under the moonlight and cheered as the town parade passed by. Although so much had changed between them, Autumn still felt a connection to Judah. Perhaps they could really be friends after all.

As they walked around the festival, Autumn and Judah were greeted with enthusiasm and warmth. Autumn noticed plenty of curious glances in their direction. She imagined folks were thinking back to the days when they'd been in love and scratching their heads at seeing them together. Most were probably just happy to see Judah participating in a community event since he'd been missing in action for years.

They stood in a short line for the fried dough where she was able to engage Judah in light chitchat. He had never been a big talker, so Autumn carried most of the conversation. Judah paid for two orders of the fried dough and they both dug in with gusto. Although it was just as delicious as she remembered, the treat was giving her a bellyache.

"I think my eyes were bigger than my stomach," Autumn said as a tight feeling spread across her abdomen. "I can't eat anymore."

"Are you all right? I seem to remember you always going for seconds on fried dough," Judah responded.

"I'm fine. Too much of a good thing," she said, scrunching up her nose. So much of the time she was fearful of something going wrong in her pregnancy. She didn't want to get paranoid about slight stomach discomfort. Doc Poppy had just given her a glowing report just days ago so she shouldn't worry. It felt a little bit like indigestion.

Judah reached for her remaining portion. "Don't mind if I do," he said, taking a huge bite.

Autumn laughed at the way he devoured the treat with such enthusiasm. He resembled a little kid. "You have some sugar on your face." She reached out and brushed it away, her fingers tingling as soon as she made contact with his skin. She was so close to him she could see the slight stubble on his chin and the little scar by his mouth. She remembered the day he'd received that scar. They had been kids hanging out in the woods and Judah had tangled with a rabid fox. She remembered watching as he got stitched up and received a rabies shot without releasing a single tear.

The lively beats of jazz music filled the air. Autumn pulled Judah by the sleeve and walked toward the platform where the band was performing. She began to clap to the upbeat rhythms as Judah stood a few feet away watching her. Suddenly, Autumn stopped in her tracks. Leif, Judah's brother, was walking straight toward them with his son, Ryan, by his side. Autumn let out a startled sound once she noticed their approach. Just when Judah seemed to be in a good place! She didn't want anything or anyone to spoil these precious moments.

Judah and Leif were on a collision course and seconds away from crossing paths. And there wasn't a thing Autumn could do to stop it from happening.

Judah hadn't imagined he would be enjoying himself so much at the festival. For the most part it wasn't

awkward running into old friends and acquaintances he
hadn't seen in quite some time. Everyone truly seemed
happy to see him again. He was glad he'd made the effort to attend rather than hole up by himself at home.
Autumn was good company, pleasant and humorous.
He couldn't help but notice the way she lovingly cra-
dled her stomach from time to time. She had so much
to look forward to, he thought. If he could, Judah would
go back in time and relive Zane's first few years and
the wonder of having a new baby in the house. Those
were precious years.

Autumn had waited a long time to have a baby, he
realized. Judah didn't have the nerve to ask her, but he
wondered why she'd decided to have a baby after all
these years. Especially in a flailing marriage. He knew
she would be an amazing mother, but there would be
challenges ahead of her. *It's none of your business!* he
reminded himself. She was living her life the way she
saw fit and he admired her courage.

Suddenly, Autumn seemed to be frozen, staring at
a spot in the distance.

"What's the matter?" he asked, following her gaze.

Leif! And Ryan. They were heading toward them
from the opposite direction, engaged in an animated
conversation. Neither one had yet spotted him. His
brother was the last person he wanted to see. He should
have known Leif would show up at the festival. There
was nothing he liked better than being in the thick of
things.

He abruptly turned toward Autumn. "I think I've had
enough of the festival."

"Judah, come on. You can't keep this up," Autumn said, grasping his wrist. "This town isn't big enough for you to not speak to one another."

Judah clenched his jaw. "It's been four years, and I've been managing just fine."

She let out an indelicate snort. "I highly doubt that."

He frowned at her. "Believe what you want."

"Isn't it time you dealt with the situation head-on?" Autumn pressed. "You don't have to be best friends, but this isn't moving forward. Isn't that what you told me earlier? That coming here today was about making progress."

Judah could see Leif continuing to walk in his direction. He stopped a few feet away from him. Judah's eyes were drawn to his nephew who was shifting from one foot to the other. Ryan glanced back and forth between Judah and his father. "Hey, Uncle Judah. Hi, Autumn. It's been a long time."

Autumn stepped toward Ryan and placed her arms around his neck, drawing him in for a hug. "I can't believe you're all grown up. And a deputy!"

"Welcome back to Serenity Peak. And congratulations on the baby," Ryan said. Before Judah knew it was happening, the two of them had walked a discreet distance away. Judah sucked his teeth. Clearly they had done so in order to allow him and Leif some privacy.

"I think it's time we talked." His brother's words came out of his mouth like a challenge. Judah immediately bristled.

"Oh, really. I thought that I made it clear that we had nothing to discuss." Judah spit out the words.

Leif took a few steps closer to him. "So you plan to go on like this for the rest of our lives? Ignoring me. Not speaking."

"Why should I? You didn't have my back when I needed you the most." Saying the words out loud caused a twisting sensation in his gut. After the accident he'd been caught up in a maelstrom of grief and pain and sadness. When he'd heard the cruel whispers about Mary being under the influence of pills the night of the accident it had brought him to his knees. He had never imagined that the people in Serenity Peak he'd known all his life could be so vicious. At one point in time Mary had been addicted to painkillers due to a chronic injury, but she had gotten clean well before Zane came into the world.

Leif scoffed. "That's not true. You've got it all twisted. Judah, grief has blinded you to reality. I never turned my back on you. I simply didn't cut off relationships with all of the folks you suspected spread rumors."

"Exactly," Judah said, breathing heavily. "I've never quite understood how you justified maintaining those friendships and business relationships."

"The key word is suspected," Leif said. "I know you were in a world of pain, but you were lashing out at everyone and anyone. It's true that a few folks were spreading terrible gossip, but it wasn't the entire town. And it was wrong of you to place blame in every direction. You didn't cut anyone an ounce of slack."

Leif's words slammed him in the face. Was his brother right? Had he taken his agony out on everyone in Serenity Peak? He had been in such deep grief four years ago. Judah hadn't known whether he was coming or going. His mind raced to find a response, but none came. A big part of him wanted to break the heavy chains he was carrying around. Anger. Resentment. Bitterness. At some point he had to acknowledge the toll these toxic emotions were taking on him as well as others.

"Why don't you admit why you're really angry at me?" Leif's voice was low and steady. Compassion flickered in his eyes.

"What are you talking about?" Judah asked.

Leif's gaze never wavered. A tremor ran alongside his jaw. "The night of the accident. That's why you've cut me out of your life. It's the reason you won't talk to me. You blame me for the crash, don't you?"

Chapter Eleven

For the last few minutes Judah had been stone silent. The encounter between him and Leif had been tense and emotional. Both of their bodies had been rigid and unyielding. They'd reminded her of two cowboys at the O.K. Corral, with neither one giving an inch to the other. Autumn hadn't meant to eavesdrop, but she'd heard Leif's voice as it carried. *You blame me for the crash.* The words had caused Autumn to shudder. What was Leif talking about?

Moments later Judah walked away from the conversation. The expression etched on his face as he walked past her had been one of shock and pain. Autumn followed behind him, knowing instinctively that he needed someone by his side. She might be overstepping, but she followed after him, trying hard to keep up with his long strides. Judah quickly reached the perimeter of the town square, away from most of the action.

"Can you slow down? Pregnant lady here," she called out. "I'm not a speed walker, especially after eating that fried dough. It's sitting on my stomach like a stone."

Judah stopped walking and looked over his shoulder at her. "You don't have to babysit me. I know this isn't exactly the fun you were expecting today."

Autumn sank down onto a bench in the town square. Judah walked back to stand next to her. "It's all right," Autumn said. "I would feel a lot better if the two of you had mended your issues, but I'm guessing that didn't happen."

"No, it didn't," he acknowledged. "But I walked away because I'm trying to process something he said to me."

She shook her head. "I never would have imagined that you and Leif would be estranged. Growing up it was rare to see one of you without the other. Don't you want to get that close bond back?" she asked. "One of the bright spots of coming back home has been the way my relationship with Cecily has strengthened. We're getting closer every day."

"Things happen, Autumn. Grief colors everything." He let out a hissing sound. "My dad would be so hurt if he was alive. I feel ashamed. He prided himself on family coming first as well as his faith. I haven't had God in my life for a while now."

Autumn knew Judah was spot-on about his dad. Kurt Campbell had been the patriarch of a loving and faith-filled family. Not only had he taught Judah everything he knew about being a fisherman, he had shown him the path to becoming a good man, rooted in faith and love.

Where had Judah's faith gone? If God was in his life, she didn't think his struggles would be so profound. Leaning on the Lord and seeking His counsel would have benefited Judah.

"It's understandable that you would question your faith after such a profound loss, but I think you need to ask yourself if you need Him in your life." Autumn wanted to be gentle and not sound judgmental. This was Judah's journey after all. She wasn't going to tell him how to live his life but she knew he would be more grounded by His presence.

"I still have a hard time processing that in one instant my whole world came crashing down around me. I've accepted it and I've walked through the grief stages, but I still wonder where was God?"

Judah's question was a deep one that she knew many struggled with after tragedies.

"I don't want to overstep, but what did Leif mean when he said you blame him for the accident?" For Autumn those words had been a bombshell. What wasn't Judah saying?

He sat down next to her and looked at the ground as he fiddled with his fingers. "The night of the accident we were over at Leif's house celebrating Ryan joining law enforcement. It was getting late and Zane was really tired. Mary had to work early the next morning so she was itching to get home." He let out a ragged sigh. "Leif wanted me to stay longer. We were looking through old photo albums and reminiscing about the past. Mary left with Zane while I stayed behind. Leif was going to take me home later on. Then the random snow and ice came…twenty minutes after they left I got the call about the crash. By the time I arrived…it was too late. They were both gone." Judah's face looked ashen and his jaw trembled.

"Oh, Judah. I'm so sorry. A living nightmare." She placed her hand over his and held it there.

"I've never really thought about it, but I guess maybe I have been blaming Leif. And I'm wrong for doing so. For the most part I've been feeling guilty about not driving my family home myself that night, but if it hadn't been for my brother—"

"You wouldn't have lost your family," Autumn said, finishing the thought for him.

"He begged me to stay that night and I did." Judah let out a brittle laugh. "I can't believe I've been holding on to this for all this time. Blaming Leif. It wasn't his fault. We were just taking a deep dive into the past with all those pictures of our family." He winced. "I never imagined that night would end in unthinkable tragedy."

"Judah, it's no one's fault. I wish you could understand that and stop thinking someone has to be responsible."

"I'm trying, Autumn. Right now I'm probably closer to accepting that reality than I've been in four years. And I know that Leif and I need to talk, just as soon as I figure out what to say to him."

"'I'm sorry' is a good start," she said. "From what I saw Leif is eager to get back on track with you. I don't think it will take much."

Judah shoved his hand through his hair. "I'll find a way. And knowing my brother, he'll never let me live this down. But it'll be worth it if we can find a way forward."

Autumn could tell Judah was ready to take this first

big step. Tears filled her eyes at the idea of reconciliation between the brothers.

"Autumn, I didn't mean to make you cry," Judah said
as he peered at her face.

"Everything makes me tear up these days," she admitted, dabbing at her eyes with the hem of her coat.
"I'm really overjoyed that you plan to make things right
with Leif." Judah's realization that he was wrong signified progress. He had managed to see the situation from
Leif's point of view. He'd gotten out of his own head
long enough to view the situation objectively.

A huge grin crept over his face. "I think my nephew
is going to be over the moon. He's been bugging me
about the situation for a long time."

"He's a wonderful young man who clearly loves his
family. I had a chance to talk to him earlier and I was
really impressed." Autumn was a firm believer that
where there was love anything was possible. She felt
incredibly hopeful about being back in Serenity Peak.
Now, more than ever she needed reassurance that she'd
made the right decision in packing up her life in New
York City to come back to Alaska.

"I'll keep you posted," Judah said, shoving his hands
in his pockets. The weather was getting chillier by the
moment with temperatures dropping. "In the meantime,
it's almost sunset. The bonfire should be starting soon
if you want to check it out."

"Of course I do," Autumn responded. She hadn't
even realized it had gotten so late, but the sky was beginning to darken. This time of year sunset was at ap-
proximately five-thirty. Because she had been away for

so many years it still took some getting used to when the sun began to fade from view.

They ran into Sean, Helene and Cecily, as well as Violet, Chase and Sky. She had been hoping they would cross paths with Leif again so Judah could begin their reconciliation. But, as with all things, she knew it would happen in God's time.

The mood amongst the townsfolk was celebratory. Kids were holding light-up wands and wearing glow-in-the-dark necklaces. S'mores were being made on the fire as the aroma of melted chocolate wafted in the air.

With the stars shining in a velvet sky and the moon illuminating the area, Autumn couldn't remember an Alaskan night quite like this one. Hope shimmered all around her. Happiness and fellowship. She couldn't explain why but it seemed as if anything was possible at this moment. Had someone told her a year ago that she would be back in Serenity Peak preparing for the birth of her first child that she would be raising alone, Autumn wouldn't have believed them. But, as she looked around the throng of people surrounding her, Autumn had a strong feeling she was meant to be here.

Judah had scored a comfy seat for her by the bonfire. By the time things got started, the area was jam-packed with townsfolk. Judah had to squeeze next to her in order to sit down. He was sitting so close to her that their arms were touching. Despite the fact that she was wearing a long-sleeved parka, Autumn shivered when Judah's arm brushed against hers. She felt a little flustered at the realization that she might be in way over her head with Judah Campbell.

Her head was telling her that Judah was off-limits, but her heart didn't seem to be listening. She needed to shake this off. He was in her past, not her future.

Judah leaned toward her, asking in a low voice, "How are you doing? Are you comfortable? I can go get you a water if you want," he offered.

His thoughtfulness had always endeared him to her. Judah was a caretaker. He was the type of man who always made sure that everyone in his sphere was taken care of. It was one of the reasons she'd fallen so hard for him. Even though Autumn felt confident in her new life in Serenity Peak, she also felt vulnerable at the moment. Being with Judah made her think of all the dreams they had once shared…marriage, kids, the white picket fence.

"I'm actually feeling really wiped out," she blurted out. "I think I'm going to head home now."

Judah's eyes widened. She thought there was a hint of disappointment on his face. "Oh, no. And miss the bonfire?"

"There's always next year," she said, standing up. As soon as the words came out of her mouth she realized that this time next year she would have a baby to take care of. Her life would be very different. Bringing a baby to a bonfire might be a stretch.

"Do you need me to walk you to your truck?" Judah asked, beginning to stand up.

"No!" she said in a raised voice. That was the last thing she needed or wanted at the moment. "I'll be fine. Goodnight," she said, quickly gathering her purse and beating a fast path away from Judah and the bonfire.

As soon as she got inside the truck, Autumn turned the ignition on and let the vehicle run until the interior warmed up. Her thoughts were all over the place and her pulse was skittering wildly. She raised her hands to her cheeks. Despite the fierce chill in the air she was flushed.

Back at the bonfire her mind had taken her to an unexpected place. The desire to kiss Judah had swept through her to the point where she'd had to walk away rather than do something foolish. A kiss would have been disastrous. And perhaps unwelcomed. They were just at the brink of becoming friends again, which meant more to her than she'd ever imagined. When it came to Judah she felt like a helpless moth drawn to a bright flame. Whenever they spent time together she found herself wanting more of him. More conversation. More laughs. More Judah. She needed to tamp down these emotions and focus on her reality—this baby she would soon be bringing into the world and her career.

There was no future for her and Judah. Autumn had burned those bridges a long time ago.

As soon as Autumn took off, Judah immediately felt a letdown in his spirits. Try as he might to enjoy the festivities, his thoughts kept veering back to Autumn. She had left the bonfire in a very abrupt manner, causing him to wonder if anything was wrong. Had he done something or said something to upset her? Was she not feeling well? Ever since Autumn had come back to Alaska Judah hadn't been able to keep her out of his mind.

It's okay to care about an ex, a little voice buzzed in his ear. *You're rebuilding a friendship and that's healthy.*

As the bonfire wound down and the crowd began to disperse, Sean cut through the crowd straight to Judah. Without skipping a beat, Sean asked, "Hey, can we talk for a minute?" Strain was evident on his face. Tiny stress lines stretched across his forehead.

"Sure, buddy. What's going on?" he asked. His first thought was about Autumn. Had something happened to her on the drive home? His heart began beating like a drum inside his chest. He knew this was a holdover from the accident four years ago. He was always waiting for impending disaster.

Sean motioned him aside. "First off, I'm so happy to see you here. It's awesome knowing you decided to take such a huge step today. Kudos."

"But?" Judah asked. He'd known Sean way too long not to know there was a *but* coming.

Sean's hands were at his sides but Judah noticed they were clenched. "What's going on with you and my sister?"

Judah sputtered. "Going on? What do you mean?"

"The two of you were hanging out all day laughing and carrying on. Then you were all cozied up at the bonfire. You obviously said something to upset her. She lit out of here like she was being chased by a grizzly bear."

The fierce expression on Sean's face caught him by surprise. It was clear Sean wasn't playing around. He meant business.

Judah held up his hands. "First of all, there's nothing going on between us other than friendship. She was gracious enough to pal around with me today. In case you forgot, I'm a little out of practice with schmoozing at town events."

"So there's nothing romantic going on?" Sean appeared to be waiting on pins and needles for his reply.

"No, there isn't," he said without hesitation. *Why did he feel as if he wasn't being completely honest?* Technically, there wasn't anything going on, but there had been loaded moments between them where he'd felt flickers of awareness. Maybe he was simply imagining things. There was absolutely no reason to say anything to Sean about those moments, especially since he and Autumn hadn't come close to crossing any lines.

"Okay, I'm sorry for grilling you and jumping to conclusions," Sean said. "It's just that she's had a hard time lately with the divorce and moving back to Serenity Peak. She doesn't let on, but she's a nervous wreck about this pregnancy. They say divorce, having a baby and relocating are three of the most stressful events in a person's life." He ran a hand across his jaw. "Autumn is undergoing all three at once."

"I get it," he said with a nod. And he did. Autumn had a lot on her plate. She was under a great deal of stress. But he had done nothing to add to her anxiety. Matter of fact, he had assisted her in finding local fishermen to interview for her article even though he'd wanted to stay out of it.

"She's pretty vulnerable right now and I don't want to see her get hurt again," Sean continued. "That husband of hers put her through a lot."

For a moment Judah was going to let the comment

slide until a little bubble of anger began to rise up inside him. What was Sean accusing him of doing? Hurt roared through him. He and Sean had been friends for most of their lives. Did he even know him at all?

"And you think I'm going to do something to hurt her?" he asked. At this point Judah wasn't even trying to keep anger out of his tone.

"Judah, I'm just trying to protect Autumn. I didn't mean to cast any aspersions on you." Even though Sean's voice was filled with remorse, Judah was still heated. Not once had he ever done a single thing to hurt Autumn. And he never would.

"In case you forgot, Autumn was the one who ended our relationship," Judah said. "She hurt me, Sean, not the other way around. I know she's your sister, but please don't act like I'm the bad guy. I would have walked through fire for that woman."

"I know, Judah. Hey, c'mon. Let's talk this out," Sean said as Judah stormed off.

Although Sean called after him Judah didn't turn back. He didn't want to stay and say something he might later regret. So much for venturing out into the community today. Two steps forward, three steps back. Maybe he should have just stayed home the way he'd been doing for the last four years. Now, he'd gotten into it with Sean, who had stuck beside him through the worst of times.

As a result of his discussion with Sean, he had yet another reason to stay away from Autumn. His best friend had just made it perfectly clear that he wasn't comfortable with them spending time together. Sean had gotten things wrong though. Judah was fairly certain that Autumn was the one who had the power to hurt him rather than the other way around.

He was more determined than ever not to allow that to happen.

Chapter Twelve

A week had passed during which Autumn hadn't laid eyes on Judah once. Nor had he texted her or called. *Ha!* She was being a bit ridiculous. It wasn't as if they had been burning up the phone lines or texting prior to this moment. And hadn't she been the one to abruptly take off from the festival? There was no telling what Judah thought of her disappearing act. As long as he didn't realize why she'd left. She would be mortified if he knew where her thoughts had drifted that night.

It didn't feel right not to hear his voice or the low rumble of his laughter. Over the past few weeks she had gotten used to him being around. He hadn't been in her life for more than a decade, yet now she missed him. If she was being honest with herself, there had been many times when she was living in New York City that she'd pined for Judah. A little voice in her head had always told her to deal with it. Their entire relationship had ended because of her choices, so she'd never allowed herself the luxury of feeling sorry for herself for long.

"You look nice. Where are you off to?" Cecily asked, giving her the once over.

In order to cheer herself up, Autumn had decided to dress up a little bit by wearing a long skirt, a silk top and her black wool coat. She planned to do a little baby shopping after her interview with Bob Agler, a retired fisherman. Bob laughingly referred to himself as an old-timer. She was meeting him at Humbled in half an hour. Once she was finished with this interview, Autumn thought she would have enough to finish the second article.

"I'm heading over to Humbled for my next interview." She rubbed her hands together. "To be honest, I'm really looking forward to sampling more of the menu over there. Everything is so delicious." She winced as pain spread across her abdomen.

Cecily reached out and grasped her by the arm. "Hey. What just happened? Are you okay?"

"I—I think so. Maybe just Braxton-Hicks contractions." As Doc Poppy had explained these contractions were the body's way of preparing for labor down the road. They didn't mean a person was actually in labor but they could be intense.

Cecily scrunched up her face. "Are you sure about that? You're barely six months along."

"Doc Poppy warned me about them. I'll definitely call her if they intensify, but I'm praying they don't. This baby needs more time in the oven," she said, chuckling.

Cecily laughed along with her. "Well, I'm heading into Northern Lights for a shift. I'm really excited to make mini Baked Alaskas today."

Autumn loved her sister's enthusiasm about her craft. She'd never seen her so excited about going to the restaurant.

"I'll love you forever if you save me some," Autumn said. Her sweet tooth had been activated by her pregnancy. After a few years of floundering, Cecily had found her life's passion.

"Done," Cecily said as she sailed out the door.

Ten minutes later Autumn was on the way to town as a light flurry of snow fell from the sky. A moose crossed the road twenty feet ahead of her. She lightly pumped the brakes so the truck wouldn't skid on the snow. Sean's truck had tire chains for safety, but driving carefully had been drummed into her growing up in Alaska. Autumn watched as the majestic animal made it across the road.

She smiled as she continued driving. How many people could say they crossed paths with an actual moose on their way to work? This, she thought, was a slice of life from Alaskan living. Being here was invigorating to her senses.

By the time she reached Humbled, Bob was already sitting at a table waiting for her. He stood up to greet her and held out a bouquet of forget-me-not flowers.

"Nice to meet you, Autumn. I remember you running around town in your younger years. Welcome back," he said with a grin.

"Thank you. I appreciate you taking the time to meet up with me."

With a shaggy mane of gray hair and a beard to match, Bob cut a striking figure. He was wearing a bow tie along with a button-down sweater. She had the feeling he'd gotten decked out for this interview.

"I'm grateful to you for writing this piece. Oftentimes we fishermen tend to be forgotten even though we're woven into the fabric of everyday Alaskan life. What we do is important."

"I couldn't agree with you more." She raised the flowers to her nose and inhaled the lovely scent. "Thank you for the flowers. How did you get them this time of year?"

He grinned at her. His green eyes sparkled. "I have a greenhouse at my home. It allows me to cultivate vegetables and flowers all year long."

For the next hour and a half, they chatted while sipping tea and nibbling on a variety of treats. Autumn's interview with Bob was informative and lively. The older man's personality was infectious. His stories about being a commercial fisherman were full of highs and lows, as well as comical moments.

"Fishing isn't just a job, Autumn. It's a way of life,"

Molly, Humbled's owner, walked up to their table just as they were finishing up. She placed her arms around Bob and said, "Hey, Grandpa. Do you need anything else?"

He lovingly patted her hand. "No, Mollygirl. We're doing just fine."

"This is your granddaughter?" Autumn asked, surprised at the connection between the two. Sometimes it seemed as if she was relearning everything about Serenity Peak all over again.

"She sure is," Bob said. He reached for Molly's hand and looked up at her. "Prettiest girl in Serenity Peak."

"Aww, you're too sweet, gramps," Molly said, her cheeks blushing.

Autumn thought that Molly and Bob might just be the most adorable twosome in town. Maybe even in all of Alaska.

As they said their goodbyes Bob reached for Autumn's hand and pressed his lips to it in an old-fashioned courtly gesture. "Until we meet again." He walked off with Molly by his side.

Autumn sat back down for a few minutes to finish her notes. When she stood up to leave she swung her large purse around so fast it caused her to stumble. Strong hands caught her before she fell. When she swung her gaze up to thank her rescuer, she saw Judah standing there.

"Judah!" she said, unable to hide her surprise. "Th-thanks for the catch. You're making a habit out of saving me."

"You're very welcome," he said. He jerked his chin in the direction of her bag. "Be careful. Your purse weighs more than you do."

"I know," she said with a smile. "I tend to overstuff my bags until they weigh a ton."

He held up a little white bag. "I came for the blueberry muffin. If you haven't tried them they're amazing."

"I'll try one next time." Autumn looked around the café. "This place is wonderful. If I didn't have errands to run, I'd happily sit here all day and try out all the different teas. Are you off today?"

Judah appeared to be looking around at everything but her. For some reason he wasn't making eye contact. "Yeah, I've been going out on the boat every day for the last week. I took today off just to get a break."

Why did it seem as if they were dancing around each other? Up to this point they had enjoyed a relatively natural ease in each other's company. Something felt completely off and she was struggling to figure it out.

All of a sudden, she didn't feel so well. Whereas a few minutes ago she'd had a slight chill, she now was experiencing hot flashes. Nausea rose up in her throat. Oh, no. She felt like she might get sick.

"Is it hot in here or is it me?" she asked. Autumn felt beads of sweat pooling on her forehead. She began to fan herself as waves of queasiness rolled through her. All of a sudden fear gripped her. Something didn't feel right. Her body began to sway to the point where Autumn worried she might fall over.

Judah gently gripped her arm in order to steady her. "What's wrong, Autumn? You don't look so good."

"Judah, I think that I need some air," she gasped. "Please, I need to go outside."

"Okay, let's go." He took her arm and gently guided her outside.

"I feel a little light-headed and nauseous. I'm feeling like I might throw up." She placed her hand low on her belly in the hopes of feeling some movement. If she could feel the baby kick then she wouldn't be so frightened. She winced as a painful cramp swept through her abdomen. *What was happening? This didn't feel right.* "I—I think something's wrong. I'm cramping." Fear had her in its grip and she choked out the words. Hot tears splashed on her cheeks.

How many nights had she prayed to make it through this pregnancy and to deliver a healthy baby? *Dear God, please don't forsake me or my child. Please shelter my baby until I can safely deliver him or her into this world.*

"Okay, don't worry. I've got you, Autumn. Let's get you to the doctor." He placed his arm around her waist and pulled her against his side so that she could place all of her weight on him.

Autumn looked up at him as she tightly clutched his side. "Judah! I'm scared. I think that I might be losing the baby."

Autumn's anguished cries were tugging at Judah's heartstrings as he broke every speed limit to transport her to the medical clinic. There hadn't been many times in his life when he had felt so helpless. Although this was very different from the crash that had taken Zane and Mary from him, he was struggling with similar emotions. Fear was leading him as well as the knowledge that at least now he had the ability to help someone he deeply cared about.

Seeing Autumn in so much pain wrecked him. He'd lost a child and he knew the utter devastation it wrought. Autumn might just snap in two under the strain if things didn't end well. She was living for this baby, her sweet blessing. If it was taken away from her it would rock her entire world. This might very well be her last chance at motherhood.

Please, Lord. Help Autumn. Give her and the baby strength enough to make it through this trial. I know You haven't heard from me in a while, but I am here now humbly asking for help.

The prayer rose up out of nowhere and surprised Judah. Where had those words come from? He hadn't been to church in four years and he never prayed. Losing his family had caused him to step away from his faith. He was still angry at God for taking away his loved ones. Not just Zane and Mary but his beloved father, Kurt. The losses had piled up one after the other, dragging him into an abyss of sorrow.

When they pulled into the parking lot, Judah put his truck in Park right by the entrance. He turned off the ignition and raced around to the passenger side door. With a quick motion, he jerked the door open and lifted Autumn out and into his arms. She didn't utter a word of protest. Autumn laced her arms around his neck and buried her face against his chest. She continued to make whimpering sounds that threatened every ounce of composure he had.

When he reached the entrance, Judah pushed the clinic door open with his elbow and made his way over the threshold.

"Help! We need some help here," Judah called out.

Staff members, followed closely by Dr. Poppy, raced to the waiting area.

"Autumn!" Poppy exclaimed as soon as she spotted her in his arms. "What happened?"

One of the nurses brought a wheelchair and placed it in front of them. Judah gently lowered her into the chair.

Autumn was groaning even louder at this point and clutching her stomach. She didn't even lift up her head to meet Poppy's gaze. "I'm cramping and nauseous. I feel hot and then cold."

"She's sick," Judah said curtly. "You need to check her out now." His voice sounded almost as frantic as he felt. Why weren't they taking her to the examination room? If Autumn was losing the baby time was of the essence.

"Excuse us, Judah," Poppy said, "but we need to assess the situation."

Autumn was tightly holding his hand. He was afraid to let go of her, but he knew the sooner he loosened his grip the faster Autumn would be examined. One of the staff wheeled her toward the back. Autumn turned and sent him a look filled with fear and anxiety. More than anything Judah wanted to reassure her that everything was going to be all right, but he couldn't shake his own fears.

What if Autumn's baby didn't make it? She would shatter into a million little pieces.

What if something happened to Autumn? He'd lost so much in his life. He wouldn't survive losing her as well.

Poppy patted his shoulder. "I promise we'll take good care of her. Will you be waiting here?" she asked.

Judah ran his hand over his face. "Yes, I'm not going anywhere. I'll be right here in the waiting room. Can you tell me if she and the baby are going to be all right?"

Poppy shook her head. "I'm sorry, but we have to

examine her and run some tests before we'll know anything. Try not to worry too much in the meantime, Judah."

That, he realized, was an impossible task. His mind was whirling with anxiety. Judah sank down onto a couch and reached into his pocket for his cell phone. He needed to let Autumn's family know what was going on. Judah quickly dialed Sean's phone number. He let out a sigh as the call went to voice mail. He looked through his contacts and found Cecily's number. He thought it was best to tell her the news so she could convey it in person to their family members.

When Cecily answered, Judah quickly told her as much as he was able to about the situation. He wished that he had more of an update to share with them.

"Poppy told me to hold tight until she can provide an update," Judah explained.

"This doesn't sound good," Cecily said. "I'll tell my parents and I'll try to get hold of Sean. Pray, Judah. Autumn and the baby need to be lifted up in prayer."

"Thanks, Cecily. I'll be in touch as soon as I know anything." Judah ended the call without saying how fervently he had been praying since the onset of Autumn's medical crisis.

For the next hour Judah paced around the waiting room, idly flipped through magazines and fielded phone calls from Autumn's family. Although they wanted to come down to the clinic, Judah advised them to stay put until the doctor provided an update. When the door opened, and the doctor began striding down the hall Judah froze. His heart was racing wildly.

Lord, please let Poppy deliver good news about Autumn and the baby.

When Poppy was within a few feet of him, a smile broke out on her face. "Autumn and the baby are going to be just fine," she said. Judah let out the ragged breath he'd been holding. All the oxygen flew out of his lungs at once.

"She's much better now that we've given her an IV. Since she hasn't been able to keep anything down we suspected food poisoning and the exam and initial tests confirm it," Poppy explained.

Food poisoning! It was rough on the body, but much less scary than where his mind had taken him. He couldn't put into words how the doctor's words made him feel. It was almost as if the weight of the world had suddenly been lifted off his shoulders.

"You can come in now and see her if you like," Poppy suggested. "I'll be back in a few minutes to check on her."

Judah walked into the room, eager to see Autumn with his own eyes. She was sitting up in the hospital bed wearing a plain blue gown. Although her complexion was a bit ashen, she looked pretty good considering what she'd been through. At the sound of his footsteps, Autumn swung her gaze toward the door.

"Hey there," Judah said as he reached her side. He jammed his hands in his pockets and shifted from one foot to the other.

"Hi," Autumn said in a soft voice. "Thanks for sticking around. It appears that I must have eaten something that made me violently ill." She wrinkled her nose and ran her hands across her abdomen. "I can't remember ever feeling such awful belly pains."

"Poppy gave me the update. You gave me quite a scare," he said. He had wanted so badly to take away her pain. That knowledge unnerved him. He was in way over his head now. And his heart was telling him it was too late to backtrack.

"I'm sorry. I was pretty petrified myself."

Seeing Autumn in so much physical agony had been difficult for Judah to witness. Her cries had done a number on his insides. He'd wanted her to lean on him so he could give her all his strength.

"Feeling better?" he asked.

"So much better," she said with a sigh. "I was so afraid that the baby was going to be in danger…or come early. Once Poppy confirmed that it was food poisoning I felt incredibly relieved."

"And the baby?" he asked. Even though Poppy had reassured him, he needed to hear it again from Autumn's lips.

"The baby seems to be fine with a strong heartbeat, but Doc is going to come back and do a sonogram just to make sure," Autumn explained. "Judah, you don't have to stay if this is dredging up painful memories for you. That's the very last thing I'd ever want to do."

He looked down for a moment as he struggled with finding the right words. "I hate medical clinics and hospital settings. I just do. That probably won't ever change. But today was different. I was actually able to help you, Autumn." He dragged his gaze up to look at her. "After the accident I rushed to the hospital, but there was nothing I could do but stare at the clinical white walls until the doctors came out and told me the terrible news. I was never able to help my family and it was the most hopeless feeling I've ever known."

Compassion flared in Autumn's eyes. He knew she understood what he'd been through which helped him get the words out.

"Don't get me wrong, I was scared for you and the baby, but knowing you're going to be fine restored me in some way. A part of me has always blamed myself for the accident that killed my family. I wasn't there to protect them and that gutted me. I should have been driving, not Mary. If I had been with them that night things would have been different."

Autumn made a fretful sound. "Oh, Judah. There wasn't anything you could have done to prevent the accident. It's impossible to turn back time and fix things. Life doesn't give us that gift."

For so long now everyone close to him had been saying the very same thing, but it hadn't resonated until now. Part of his grief had been rooted in guilt. Finally, he was in a place where he could clearly see he wasn't to blame. Accidents were by nature unpredictable and chaotic. And in order to move forward he had to accept that he couldn't change the events of that tragic night.

"It's been a long time coming, but I realize that now," he admitted. "It's finally sinking in."

Because of you, he wanted to say. So much of his personal growth as of late could be tied to Autumn's return to town. He was opening up and letting his guard down. He was realizing that he needed to be a part of the Serenity Peak community. Being at the Midnight Sun festival had shown him that. No man *was* an island. He required God in his life. And Autumn. Sweet, beautiful Autumn. His first love. His friend. A woman he couldn't get out of his mind. Or his heart.

Just as Judah opened his mouth to let her know how deeply he cared about her, the door opened with a sharp click, putting an abrupt halt to his near confession.

Chapter Thirteen

The door swung open and Doc Poppy reentered the examination room. Autumn had the distinct feeling that Judah had been on the verge of telling her something important. But whatever he'd wanted to say had been swallowed up by the doctor's arrival.

Judah's presence was reassuring. She didn't know what she would have done if he hadn't been at Humbled when she'd fallen ill. It was nice watching his evolution from a man shrouded in pain and loss to one who was now pushing past grief to make a life for himself and to care for others.

"I'm back. Sonogram time," Poppy called out. "Let's see what this little one is up to in there."

Judah looked back and forth between them. "Should I leave and give you some privacy?" he asked. The sheepish expression stamped on his face was comical, Autumn thought. He really was such a sweetheart.

"There's nothing invasive about this," Poppy responded. "I'm just putting some gel on her stomach before waving the wand around her abdomen so we can get a clear view of the baby. Nice and easy."

Judah turned to look at Autumn. "I'd like you to stay if it's not too much trouble," she said. She hated putting him on the spot, but Judah's presence gave her strength. He'd been so calm and reassuring during her medical crisis.

"Let's do this," Judah said, sending her an encouraging nod.

Within seconds Poppy had everything set up. Autumn sat back patiently as gel was spread on her abdomen and the process began. A whooshing sound filled the air as Poppy pointed to a small shape on the screen. She began to point out body parts. Head. Spine. Fingers. A pulsing heartbeat.

Tears streamed down Autumn's face, and she made no attempt to wipe them away. These were born out of joy and she honestly couldn't remember the last time that had happened. The last few hours had brought her so much fear and anxiety, as well as physical discomfort. Relief washed over her. Suddenly, all was right in her world.

"I can't believe I'm actually seeing my little peanut," Autumn said. This, she thought, was the embodiment of all the dreams she'd nurtured about bringing a life into the world.

"I can tell you the gender if you want to know," Poppy said, smiling at her. "It's your choice. Some people like to be surprised."

"Please tell me," Autumn instructed. "No more surprises for me. After what I went through today I want to know who's in there." She let out a nervous giggle. Either way, all she wanted was a healthy child.

"It's a boy," Poppy announced.

Autumn let out a little squeal. She couldn't take her eyes off the screen. Her beautiful baby boy! He was safe and sound. *Thank you, Lord, for answering my prayers.*

"Congratulations," Judah said, reaching out and squeezing her hand.

"So I'll print a copy of the ultrasound for you," Poppy said as she wiped the gel off Autumn's abdomen. "I'd like to see you next week just to follow up with you. For the next few days just relax and hydrate. You'll be back to normal in a few days."

Judah left the room so Autumn could get changed into her street clothes and ditch the hospital gown. A short while later they were in Judah's truck, and he was driving her home. Cecily and Sean had already picked up her vehicle from Fifth Street. When they pulled up, Cecily's house was ablaze with lights.

"Looks like people are waiting on you," Judah said. "It's lit up like a Christmas tree." He wondered if Sean was inside. They still hadn't spoken since the festival.

"That's sweet of them. Thanks for telling my family not to come check on me at the clinic. My parents don't need that kind of stress. I hate that I worried everyone," Autumn said. "But it's also comforting to know I'm not alone."

He reached out and grazed his palm across her cheek. "You were really brave, Autumn. I know it must have been scary in the moment, but you handled everything like a champ."

She heaved a tremendous sigh. "I was really scared, but you guided me through the worst parts of the whole ordeal. I can't thank you enough."

"I wouldn't have wanted to be anywhere else," he murmured. "I'm so happy that the two of you are fine."

Looking into Autumn's eyes was like tumbling down a rabbit hole. He could see a wealth of emotion radiating from their depths. There was nothing he wanted more in this moment than to kiss her. Despite all of his past doubts, he couldn't think of a single reason why he shouldn't. *Seize the moment.*

He moved closer then dipped his head down and placed his lips on hers. Judah tenderly placed his mouth over hers, enjoying the sweet taste of her. Her lips tasted like spun sugar. The moment their lips touched Judah felt sparks flying all around them. Her lovely floral scent rose to his nostrils. She placed her arms around his neck and pulled him closer, drawing him further into the kiss. Judah wanted the embrace to go on and on until the stars were stamped from the sky.

She whispered his name against his lips just before they broke apart. Judah leaned his forehead against Autumn's for a few beats. They were still so closely connected he could hear the steady pulsing of her heart. He placed one last kiss on her temple before saying, "You should get some rest. It's been a long day."

Her hands were still clutching the collar of his parka. When she let go, Judah wanted to reel her back in. He wanted to hold Autumn in his arms and protect her from anything that might cause harm to her. Because once they drew apart, he knew the doubts would creep back in.

He quickly stepped down from the truck and made his way to the passenger side. Once he opened the door, Judah held out his hand and helped Autumn out. Although under normal circumstances he would walk her to the door, Judah didn't want to exacerbate the situation with Sean. For all he knew, his best friend could be upset that Judah had been the one to take her to the clinic.

"Night, Judah," Autumn said in a low voice.

"Night," he said, turning on his heel and heading back to the truck. For a few moments he sat and watched Autumn as she walked to the door and let herself in. For a moment he'd had the impression she had wanted one last kiss before they parted ways. Her beautiful face had been turned upward toward him. Judah didn't know how to explain it, but stepping outside the truck into the chilly night air had woken him up a bit. He had been in a bit of a dreamy state when he had initiated the kiss.

On the drive back to his place, Judah kept thinking that kissing Autumn had been one of the most foolish things he could have done. Not that their embrace hadn't been fantastic. Autumn had responded with such tenderness and longing. Smooching Autumn had felt so right in the moment, but it hadn't taken long for doubt to creep in. Autumn wasn't the type of woman to kiss as a spur of the moment whim. And now, he wondered if he was giving out mixed signals.

They were friends and nothing more, despite the way she stirred up old feelings inside of him. Romance only complicated things. He didn't think he could handle a full-fledged relationship with Autumn. He questioned whether he could ever fully trust her not to crush his heart again. In their past he had been over the moon for her, and it was unlike anything he had ever felt for anyone else.

So many years had gone by since they'd been in love. It was a long time to be apart from someone. Over the years Autumn had blossomed into a wiser and more confident woman. Witnessing her being so excited about welcoming her baby boy into the world had touched his heart in ways he couldn't even explain. Back at the clinic he'd watched as Autumn's baby flashed on the screen. Such a tiny blessing. A perfect creation. Yet he had experienced a mix of emotions. He'd been ecstatic that Autumn's medical crisis had been something easily treatable. Her joy had been effusive. Yet it had been hard to see the baby boy on the screen. He and Mary had sat in a doctor's office and viewed their baby on the same type of screen. They had both been overjoyed by the sight of their healthy, robust baby boy.

How could Autumn ever truly understand that he was grappling with his emotions about her little blessing? She would be terribly hurt. It made him feel awful, but he couldn't pretend that his feelings didn't exist.

Being around her was wonderful, but terrifying at the same time. She had shattered his heart once before and he couldn't trust that she wouldn't break it all over again.

As soon she stepped inside the house Autumn was swept up in the loving arms of her family. Her parents were the first ones to step forward and wrap her in a tight embrace. Raw emotion radiated from them in waves.

"We're so relieved to see you," her mother said. "We didn't want to think the worst, but when Cecily called us we were beside ourselves."

"We sent up a lot of prayers," her dad told her. His voice cracked as he barely got the words out.

"And got down on our knees." Her mother crossed her hands in prayerlike fashion. "It's such a blessing to know our daughter and grandbaby are doing well."

"Come sit down. You shouldn't be on your feet," her father said, guiding her toward the living room.

Cecily and Sean looked on with wide grins as their parents fussed over her. Autumn didn't balk at all the tender love and care they were showing her. It felt nice to be looked after even though she was an adult now and ready to mother her own child.

"Let her up for air," Sean said. "You're smothering her."

A half an hour later her parents and Sean headed home after reminding Autumn to get a good night's rest and drink plenty of water. As soon as they left Cecily led her to the kitchen for a nice cup of decaf green tea and some crackers.

"Hopefully you'll be able to keep this down," Cecily said. "Make sure to eat the crackers slowly." Autumn was seeing such a nurturing side of her sister. She would make a wonderful mother herself.

"So you and Judah, huh," Cecily said. She wiggled her brows in Autumn's direction.

"Not so fast. We're just friends," Autumn said. But did friends make out in trucks? She didn't think so.

"So you haven't kissed at all?" her sister asked, her voice filled with disappointment.

"Just once," she admitted. "Tonight actually."

Cecily let out a squeal of delight. "I knew something was brewing. The two of you have that whole meant-to-be vibe."

Autumn bit her lip. "I'm not sure that's true. It's complicated. Judah acted a bit aloof after we kissed. And it's not as if we declared any feelings for one another." She shrugged. "It's a bit up in the air."

"But you do feel something for him, right?" Cecily leaned across the counter using both elbows. She was waiting with bated breath for Autumn's answer.

"Yes," she said, nodding. "There's so much I'm feeling for him, but it just seems like our past is still casting this shadow over us."

"What do you mean? There's really nothing standing in your way."

"Oh, Cecily, that's not true." She took a deep breath. "I never wanted to end things with Judah in the first place."

Cecily's eyes widened. "Then why did you? At the time you made it seem as if you'd outgrown him."

"That wasn't the case. Not at all. I only broke up with him after I was told that I couldn't bear children."

Cecily let out a gasp and raised a hand to her neck. "What are you talking about?"

"My endometriosis diagnosis was twelve years ago. Because I had so many polyps I was told by my gynecologist that it would be impossible for me to conceive a child." Tears streamed down her face. She let out a little hiccup. "I knew how much Judah wanted children.

He talked about raising a houseful of kids all the time. Whenever he was around kids he lit up like sunshine. How could I take that away from him? I made a sacrifice so he could live the life of his dreams."

Cecily couldn't hide her shock. "Why didn't you tell me? I would have told you not to do it. You could have adopted or fostered. Or you could have just told him the truth and dealt with it head-on."

How many times over the years had she told herself the same exact things? Back then her mind hadn't been in that headspace. She'd been lost and confused and grieving the loss of what might have been.

"Yes, I know that now," she acknowledged. "But at the time I was so broken after being given that news. It felt as if my entire life was crumbling right along with Judah's. We had so many hopes and dreams that revolved around getting married and having children. I knew he was thinking of proposing to me." She twisted her fingers around and around. "It seemed as if I was ruining everything we'd planned. And I couldn't have stood it if he stayed with me out of pity. So I set him free."

She let out a sob filled with regret and despair. Her past actions were indefensible.

Cecily came around the kitchen island and put her arms around Autumn. "Oh, sweetie. You were so young and uncertain. You did what you thought was right at the time. But if you and Judah want to start fresh, that's still possible."

"There's no way we could ever be together until I

come clean with Judah. And even then, I have no idea if he can ever forgive me."

Cecily patted her back. "Don't give up hope. Wait and see if the two of you are on the same page about your feelings. If so, you can find a way to tell Judah the truth. If he cares for you as I think he does, he'll forgive you."

Autumn sniffed back tears. Cecily was right. She didn't even know for certain where Judah's heart lay. For him, their kiss might have been nothing special or just a way to pass the time. Either way, she knew the truth was important. This lie of omission had festered for way too long already. It would eat her alive if she kept quiet. She had come back to Serenity Peak for a fresh start and to live her life in peace and comfort. That was still her goal. Being honest with Judah would establish a strong foundation for the future.

Lord, please help me find a way to speak the truth. Give me the courage to follow through with my intentions. And if Judah can't understand my motivations, grant me the grace to understand his feelings.

Judah looked out over Kachemak Bay and breathed in a contented breath. In all the world there couldn't be a more stunning view than Serenity Peak Harbor. The sun was dipping below the horizon, casting an orange glow in its wake. Being a fisherman wasn't an easy profession by any means, but Judah loved it. His body was bone-tired, but his mind felt free of all the things that had been weighing him down for the past few years. That was the power of the Bay. It was soul soothing and life affirming. Today it had allowed him to think about his future…and Autumn.

In a few minutes he would be meeting up with Leif, at Judah's invitation. He'd reached out to his brother yesterday in an attempt to clear the air between them and they'd arranged for Leif to come down to the boat. His nerves were on edge in anticipation of their upcoming discussion. *What if they couldn't bridge the gap?*

"Thanks, boss."

"See you tomorrow."

"Take it easy, captain." His crew called out to him before they gathered up their belongings. Judah watched as his crew dispersed and headed home to eat and sleep. They would return in the wee hours of the morning to do it all over again. It was exhausting but rewarding work. There wasn't a single crew member who didn't pull their weight. That single fact made him proud.

He stayed behind to clean the boat and spray down the holds. He stripped off his GORE-TEX jacket, bibs and rubber boots, packing them away for tomorrow's work day before putting on his winter parka. A quick glance at his watch was interrupted by the sound of footsteps on the dock. His brother was right on time!

Judah looked up and Leif was standing a few feet away from him. Sometimes when he looked at his brother it was almost like looking into a mirror. The resemblance was uncanny. Growing up they had always been mistaken for twins. Irish twins—born less than a year apart—their mother had always said.

"Need some help?" Leif offered, moving closer.

"Thanks, but I'm pretty much done," Judah said. He

shouldn't be nervous, but he was. This is Leif, he reminded himself. You know each other inside and out.

Leif swept his gaze around the boat. "It's been a long time since I've been here. You run a tight ship," he said. "Dad would get a kick out of that."

Judah smiled. *You run a tight ship.* That had always been their father's favorite expression and the highest compliment one could ever receive. Hearing those words come out of Leif's mouth highlighted one of the things that would always bind them together. They were family. And somehow, out of blindness, he had forgotten the raw power of those connections.

"So, you asked me to meet you here." His gaze narrowed. "You either want to talk or you're going to throw me overboard. Which is it?"

"I'm sorry." He swallowed hard. Apologizing wasn't difficult but there was so much he needed to say. *Where did he even start?* "I was a fool to cut you out of my life, Leif. There's so much I want to say, but it might take me forever to get it all off my chest. You were right. I didn't realize how much I was holding onto until the festival. On some level I've been blaming you for asking me to stay that night." He shoved his hands into his pockets. "It allowed me to think that maybe I could have saved them if only I had gone home with Mary and Zane. And it placed the blame on you rather than on me, because living with the guilt has been almost too much to bear."

"There's absolutely nothing to feel guilty about," Leif said. "I wish you could accept that as the truth."

"My head knows that on some level, but my heart tells a different story."

Leif stood quietly and listened. "We've lost a lot of time, Judah. I don't want to dwell on fault or blame. Tomorrow isn't promised. All I really care about is that we're in a good place moving forward. I've missed you."

"I'll do my part to make that happen," Judah promised. "I've missed having you around."

"I know what you've been through...what you've lost. You've been knocked down, Judah, but you got up. You didn't give in to despair. I think you're pretty brave," Leif said, tearing up. "God isn't through with you yet. He has great plans for you."

Judah took a step toward Leif, easily closing the distance between them. He grabbed his brother by the shoulders and pulled him into a bear hug. The heartfelt embrace went on for a long time. Judah didn't want to let go and he sensed Leif was of the same mind. By the time they pulled apart both had moisture pooling in their eyes.

Leif cleared his throat. "So...you and Autumn looked mighty cozy at the festival. Anything going on there?" Leif raised an eyebrow.

Judah couldn't act cavalier with Leif. His brother knew him too well for him to pull that off. "I have feelings for her, Leif. From the moment our paths crossed again, I've been pulled in her direction like a magnet. She's just as gorgeous and lively as she was when we were together. And she might be the most interesting woman I've ever known."

"And she's having a baby?" Leif asked. "Ryan mentioned it."

Judah smiled. "Yes. A boy. And she couldn't be any more excited about welcoming a child into the world."

Leif knitted his brows together. "Is that a complication for you?"

He weighed his words carefully. His feelings had been all over the place. "Honestly, I wasn't sure. I was with her when she found out that she was having a boy. I was torn between excitement and fear." A sigh slipped past his lips. "That sounds awful, but Zane's death is still raw. Maybe it always will be."

"It doesn't sound awful. Just honest."

"We kissed last week, but neither of us has said anything about where we go from here. For all I know she doesn't feel the same way that I do." That thought gutted him. Maybe he was reading everything wrong.

Leif chuckled. "Judging from what I saw at the festival you don't need to worry. She's smitten."

Although Leif's assessment made him stand a little taller, he was still unsure. "I've been wondering if I can trust her which might not be fair. We were much younger then and if she wasn't certain about me, can I really hold it against her?"

"Sounds like you're pretty stuck on her," Leif said with a knowing look. "Those old feelings are still there. Don't put roadblocks in your way."

Judah shifted from one foot to the other and ran a weary hand across his face. His brother was right. "I did a lot of thinking today when I was out on the boat. I've spent the last four years steeped in grief and pain. I cut you out of my life as well as God. Not to mention the townsfolk. Having a second chance with Autumn is my rainbow after the storm. I don't want to blow it."

"So what are you going to do about it?" his brother asked.

Leif knew how to challenge Judah like no one else on earth.

"I'm going to tell her what's resting on my heart," Judah said. A burst of confidence flooded him. Up until now he'd been filled with so many doubts and insecurities.

Leif held up his hand for Judah to high-five. As the brothers celebrated Judah's decision to be open and honest with Autumn, he couldn't help but feel that his life was changing for the better. Finally, he was coming out of the shadows and embracing the sunlight.

Chapter Fourteen

Autumn woke up to a beautiful Alaskan morning. The sky was the color of forget-me-nots, the state flower of Alaska. The sun was dazzling in a sky almost devoid of clouds. She was on her way to Northern Lights to pick up Cecily. The thought of running into Judah there crossed her mind, but he was most likely fishing today. A smile tugged at her lips at the memory of the day she'd spent out on the water with Judah and his crew. She would love to go out on the Bay with him again, although she wasn't confident it would happen.

She wasn't quite sure what to think about Judah. He had done a little bit of a disappearing act on her and it was confusing. Ever since the night they had kissed, he'd been radio silent. Autumn had been left to wonder if he was avoiding her. They had bonded so beautifully during her medical ordeal. He had been so tender and supportive.

Had she said or done something to push him away? Did he regret kissing her?

It was hard not to feel hurt that he hadn't checked in on her. Had she been imagining them growing closer to the point where both of them were feeling more than friendship? Surely a kiss meant something. But perhaps it had caused Judah to run for the hills.

She was trying to stop fretting about Judah. It was time to shift her focus to practical matters. She still needed so many items for the baby's arrival. A crib. Diapers. A bassinet. Cecily had offered to go with her into town so they could do a little baby shopping. The day of her medical crisis she'd never made it to the shops, so in her mind she was way overdue some retail therapy.

When she pulled up outside the restaurant Autumn put the truck in Park then texted Cecily to let her know she'd arrived. She knew if she went inside it would only prolong their departure since the customers who frequented Northern Lights tended to be chatty. It would take her forever to get out of there.

A strong gust of wind swept inside the truck as the passenger side door swung open. Instead of Cecily it was Judah stepping up into the passenger side seat.

"Hey there, beautiful," Judah said with a wide grin.

"Judah! What are you doing here?" She wasn't even annoyed at him anymore for leaving her hanging after their kiss. With just one look at his handsome face Autumn forgot all about the way she'd been feeling for the past few days. Chills were racing down the back of her neck at his close proximity.

"I have a surprise for you!" His blue eyes sparkled. He resembled a little kid at the moment with the gleeful expression stamped on his face.

"Really?" she asked. "More surprising than popping into my ride when I was expecting my sister?" She shook her head in disbelief. Although he had been on her mind a lot, she hadn't expected this sudden turn of events.

He looked at her earnestly. "I know you had plans with Cecily, but there's something really cool I need to show you. Please don't be mad at her. This is all me. She just went along with the plan."

A secret plan? This really wasn't Judah's style. He wasn't an impulsive person. Or at least the old version of Judah hadn't been. The man sitting next to her in the passenger seat was full of surprises.

"Okay, so where to?" Autumn was stepping out on a limb of faith and trusting Judah. What did she have to lose? She would have to postpone her baby shopping for another time.

Judah proceeded to give her step-by-step directions. A short while later they were on the back roads leading away from town and toward the mountains. Even though her mind was whirling with ideas about their final destination, Autumn took time to soak in the view. Serenity Peak's mountains and wildlife sightings were a far cry from the skyscrapers and throngs of people in New York City.

All of a sudden Autumn knew exactly where they were headed. Sugar Works. They had just driven past the hot springs, so the only other big location in this area was the Drummonds' property. She wondered if Violet was in on this as well.

"What do you have up your sleeve?" She darted a

quick glance in his direction when she slowed the car down at a bear crossing sign.

He made a turning the key motion near his lips. "I'm not saying a word until we get there. There aren't many happy surprises in life, so why not savor the anticipation?"

"When you put it like that," Autumn said, "I'll just focus on the road and enjoy not knowing what's happening."

The low rumble of Judah's laugher filled the interior of the truck. By this time Autumn wasn't even listening to Judah's directions. She knew how to get to Sugar Works by heart. When she turned in to the lane leading to the property, Judah told her exactly where to go. As she drove up to the red barn a sign announcing "Abel's Place" greeted them.

"Curiouser and curiouser," Autumn said. She placed the car in Park and turned toward Judah. "So…we're here. Want to clue me in on what you're up to?"

"Sure thing, but I need to show you," Judah said, jerking his chin in the direction of the barn.

"You didn't get me a puppy did you?" Although she loved furry four-legged friends, Autumn didn't think the timing was right for her to bring a dog into her life. She would be up to her elbows in dirty diapers and baby food.

"No, I didn't get you a puppy," Judah said. "Let's get out of the truck before your imagination really starts to run wild."

Once they exited the truck, Abel came walking

out of the barn. He was wearing a white apron, a long T-shirt, jeans and workman's gloves.

"Hey, Abel. How's it going?" Judah called out to the older man.

"Pretty well. I've been waiting for the two of you to get here," Abel said as he enveloped Autumn in a hug.

"It's good to see you, Abel, even though I'm in the dark as to what we're doing here," Autumn said as she looked back and forth between the two men. "Anyone care to tell me?"

"Well, come on inside the barn and all will be revealed," Abel said. His eyes were twinkling with merriment. He seemed quite pleased with himself.

Judah pulled the barn door open and ushered her inside. Once Autumn entered, the smell of wood shavings permeated the air. Everywhere she looked were examples of Abel's woodworking skills. A beautiful mahogany chair. A jewelry box. A small dresser.

Abel led them toward the corner where an object sat covered with a large tarp.

"I'll let you do the honors," Abel said, nodding toward Judah, who quickly went to stand beside the covered object.

"Autumn, this is a gift for you and the baby. Crafted with love." Judah ripped the tarp away, revealing a stunning maple-colored crib. The wood sparkled and glistened. The craftsmanship was immaculate. Along the headboard were grooves in the shape of clouds.

Autumn stood without moving a muscle, transfixed by the site of the magnificent crib. After a few moments she walked over and lovingly ran her hand across the headboard. "This is for me?" she asked. She couldn't believe it!

"It is. And the baby of course," Judah said with a smile. "I asked Abel about making a crib for you, but it wouldn't have been ready for quite some time. Coincidentally, he happened to be working on one that he was willing to sell to me. I actually suggested some of the little details on the headboard. I thought little clouds would help him sleep better."

"This is such a beautiful surprise," she gushed. "Abel, thank you for creating something so stunning. I feel incredibly blessed that my baby boy will be sleeping in this work of art."

"All the thanks should go to Judah," Abel said. "He was determined to make sure you received the perfect crib for your baby." He chuckled. "He hounded me a bit to make sure I was on schedule. Okay, if you'll excuse me, I need to head over to give a tour of the property." Before they knew it, Abel had sailed through the barn doors, leaving them alone.

Autumn was awash in gratitude. She hadn't been expecting such a magnificent gesture "How can I ever thank you, Judah? This truly means so much to me. It's really exquisite."

"You don't need to thank me. Consider it a baby gift and a welcome back to Serenity Peak gift all rolled into one."

"I'm grateful, Judah. It may very well be the most wonderful blessing I've ever received. Other than the baby of course." She was getting choked up at the idea that Judah had arranged something so special for her and the baby. And here she had been wondering if he cared about her. Surely this wondrous offering meant something.

"Can you hold the barn door open for me? I should get this packed up."

"Sure thing," Autumn said, striding over to the doors and swinging them wide open.

Judah picked up the medium-size crib and carried it to the truck, then placed it down on the ground while Autumn pulled the hatch down. Within a few minutes the crib was safely secured in the back of the truck.

Autumn gazed at the gift. She still couldn't believe that Judah had been so thoughtful. "I hope you know that I might never stop thanking you for the crib."

"You and the baby deserve everything good this world has to offer. I'm just happy that I was able to help you in some way."

She wanted to know where they stood. Was the crib a kind gesture from a friend...or something more? What was the point in holding her tongue? At least this way she would know.

"I was surprised to see you earlier at Northern Lights. I had the impression you were avoiding me. I could be wrong, but it felt like you had mixed emotions about the kiss we shared." She let out the breath she'd been holding. A sense of relief flooded her. It felt good to get this off her chest.

"It wasn't the kiss. Our past is complicated. I'm still a work in progress in case you hadn't noticed. You have the baby as your main priority, as he should be. There's a lot of moving pieces, Autumn. But I care for you...

deeply. Ever since you came back to town you've never been far from my thoughts."

"That's good to know," she murmured. Happiness gave her wings. She felt as if she could soar at this very moment.

"So as not to leave any doubt about how I feel about smooching you…" Judah reached out and placed his hands on the sides of Autumn's neck, pulling her close. He leaned down and put his lips over hers, tenderly showing her what her heart already knew.

Autumn kissed him back with equal measure, resting her hand over his thumping heart. She wondered if it always beat so fast or was this a result of their embrace? The smell of birch syrup drifted on the wind as the kiss soared and crested. Judah ran his hands through her hair and after they pulled apart he continued to rain kisses on her temple, cheeks and by her earlobe.

The other embrace had been wonderful, but this one signified something she'd needed to know. Judah had feelings for her and kissing her wasn't something he questioned any longer. Being swept away by Judah really was like coming home again. He had always been the big love of her life and now she knew without a shadow of a doubt that they were rekindling their romance. She didn't know if this relationship would withstand the test of time, but she was beginning to believe it might have staying power.

Everything in her life was falling into place, yet her lie of omission still stood between them. Judah deserved to know everything she had withheld from him in the past. She opened her mouth but the words wouldn't come. A new life with Judah was within reach, but opening up to him could cost her everything.

"Ready to head back to town?" Judah asked as his fingers stroked her earlobe.

"I'm ready," she answered, locking gazes with Judah. There was so much radiating from his eyes that mirrored her own feelings—joy, wonder and hope.

Please, God, she prayed. *Let the shadows of the past fade away so that we can build a solid foundation for a future.*

As happy as she was, Autumn couldn't quiet the loud whisper in her head on the ride back to town. It reminded her that until she spoke complete truth to Judah, everything they were building sat on shaky ground that could easily tumble down around her.

As far as Judah was concerned, life was pretty good. Earlier this morning he'd gone to church with Autumn. It was the first time he had been back in four years. He had surprised himself by singing along to every hymn and thoroughly enjoying himself. All this time he hadn't made the connection that God not being present in his life was responsible for the gaping hole at his center. Attending Sunday service had served as a healing balm. He still had work to do, but he was walking a righteous path.

Now he was grabbing lunch with Leif and Sean at Northern Lights before meeting up with Autumn later on to watch a movie.

"So how are things going with Serenity Peak's newest It Couple?" Leif asked.

"I can't complain," Judah said. "Everything's going smoothly. We're falling back into familiar rhythms which is uncanny considering it's been a while."

"Pretty smooth move with the crib," Sean said with a nod of approval. "Autumn can't stop talking about it. Abel really outdid himself. And so did you, Judah." Sean held out his hand so he could fist bump Judah.

Judah and Sean had managed to talk things through with Judah acknowledging that he and Autumn were more than friends. He'd promised Sean that no matter what happened he would never hurt Autumn. He loved her too much. Judah hadn't said those words yet to Autumn, but he knew it was time. Sometimes when they were together Judah wanted so badly to profess his love to her, but he always held back. A part of him wondered if the past didn't still have him in its grip. Was he afraid of Autumn hurting him all over again?

Fear thou not, for I am with thee. The passage from Isaiah washed over him with the strength of a thousand suns. Going forward, this would be his mantra. He wasn't going to let fear rob him of his future. He needed to believe in his and Autumn's potential. It was limitless.

Judah drummed his fingers on the table. "I want to make Autumn happy. Seeing her smile is my happy place."

Leif and Sean began groaning loudly. "You've got it bad," Leif said. "That was like a cheesy greeting card."

Sean was chuckling. "Seeing you like this is hilarious."

Judah didn't mind the ribbing. "I'm happy. If that

makes me corny then so be it. Autumn doesn't seem to mind."

"You tell 'em," Cecily said as she walked up with a tray of desserts. "I'm testing out some new recipes so I wanted the three of you to be the first to try them."

Sean rubbed his hands together. "Mmm. You don't have to ask me twice."

"You're in for a treat, Leif," Judah said.

"We've got a chocolate Alaskan moose tart, a pecan cinnamon pound cake and key lime cupcakes," Cecily explained as she placed the servings in front of them. "When you get a moment, let me know which one is your favorite and least favorite."

Leif's eyes widened as he dug into the pound cake. He closed his eyes and said, "Oh, this is incredible. Marry me, Cecily!" he said, placing his hand over his heart.

Cecily giggled. "That good, huh? You're going to have to get in line, Leif Campbell. Half of the single men in town are proposing once they've tasted my desserts. Including your son."

All three men burst out laughing. As Cecily headed back toward the kitchen they continued to enjoy their lunch and the dessert samples.

After finishing lunch, Judah headed back to his house to check in on Delilah and take her for a long walk. The weather forecast for this evening predicted a small storm later this evening. Judah made sure to put more salt down around his walkway and steps. Before heading over to meet up with Autumn, he fed the Irish Setter and made sure she had plenty of water to tide her over. "I'll see you later, girl. Next time I'll bring you with me, okay?"

As he headed over to Cecily's house Judah's mind began to whirl regarding all the things he didn't know about Autumn. *How did she take her coffee in the morning? Did she want a dog of her own one day? Was her favorite color still pink?*

It was exciting being on this journey of discovery with Autumn. Little by little they would peel back the layers until there wasn't anything they didn't know about one another. Pretty soon they would be finishing each other's sentences like back in the day. God had blessed them by reuniting him and Autumn. He wasn't going to take it for granted because he knew people didn't usually get second chances.

Chapter Fifteen

Autumn walked around the kitchen making sure she had everything set for this evening. A hearty beef stew was cooking in her Crock-Pot while sourdough bread baked in the oven. The aroma wafting around the house was mouthwatering.

Sweet, wonderful Judah. She had so much to be thankful for, with the baby and Judah being at the top of her list. She enjoyed spending time with him. They were at ease in each other's presence. Judah had allowed God back into his life and she knew it had altered his outlook. Being able to lean on the Lord in times of turmoil was a game changer.

She was more optimistic about her future than she could ever remember. And Judah was a huge part of it all.

Reality check! They couldn't walk off into the sunset any time soon. Her lie still stood between them. She had conveniently pushed it to the back of her mind for weeks now, but doing so didn't change anything. Judah still didn't know that she had ended things with him in a misguided attempt to spare him a life without children. He had no clue that she had dealt with an infertility diagnosis.

What difference does it make now? a little voice buzzed in her ear. *He never has to know. Just stuff it down into a little black hole.*

But *she* would know. And if she did end up with Judah in a permanent way, that lie of omission would burn a whole straight through her heart. There was no doubt about it. She wouldn't be able to live with herself.

How many times had she bashed herself for going down that road in the first place? Judah trusted her and he had no idea that she didn't deserve his faith in her. Why hadn't she listened to Violet twelve years ago when she had begged Autumn to tell Judah the truth? Her heart had been in the right place, but not divulging everything to Judah had been the wrong decision. And tonight she would have to face it head-on. It was time to do what was right.

When Judah walked into the house an hour later, Autumn was a bundle of nerves. She had no way of knowing how this night would end. Either in tears or in triumph.

Judah sniffed the air. "Something smells incredible. You Hines women sure know your way around a kitchen," Judah said.

"I can't take much of the credit for the beef stew. The Crock-Pot is doing all the work."

He placed his arm around her waist and brought her close so that their bodies were touching. Judah leaned in and kissed her. It was short and sweet, but full of tenderness.

"I missed you."

She shook her head and chuckled. "How is that possible? We went to church together this morning."

"I don't know, but it's the truth," Judah said. "I promise."

"If I'm being completely honest, I missed you too," Autumn admitted.

"The good thing is," Judah said, "there's absolutely no reason why we have to miss each other ever again."

Autumn nodded in agreement. Her throat suddenly felt as dry as a desert.

"Let's eat," she suggested, leading Judah toward the table. She had already set the table and added utensils, floral placemats and her sister's best china, as well as crystal glasses.

Judah let out an appreciative whistle. "You really went all out."

"Why don't you sit down while I get our bowls," she said, then headed back to the kitchen for the beef stew and the sourdough bread. When she returned Autumn placed the food on the table before joining hands with Judah and saying grace.

They ate in companionable silence, interrupted only by Judah's compliments about the meal. Autumn ate slowly, knowing that her moment of reckoning was quickly approaching. As they finished the food, Autumn picked up the plates and brought them to the kitchen. Although she had tried to keep Judah seated, he ended up following her to the kitchen and helping her fill the dishwasher with the dirty dishes.

After finishing up they settled in to the TV room to watch the movie. Autumn was so nervous about talking to Judah that she had completely forgotten what movie they had decided to watch. All she knew was that it was a thriller starring Sandra Bullock. They got comfy on the couch with two canned sodas.

Autumn couldn't enjoy herself. It felt wrong to pretend as if nothing was wrong when in reality so much was resting under the surface. But now it was all bubbling up. She couldn't bury it any longer.

"Judah, we need to talk," Autumn blurted before she could chicken out.

Judah's jaw went slack. "I don't think any man in history has been happy to hear those words. This must be important if you're preempting our viewing of *Maximum Speed*." He smiled when he said it so she knew he was joking, but she didn't have the strength to joke back.

"Before I say anything else, I just want to let you know that I love you."

Autumn's voice sounded strong and sure when she professed her love to him. Was this what she wanted to talk to him about? If so, he would be the happiest man on earth.

Love! Autumn's words sent him to the stratosphere. He didn't think his feet were even touching the ground anymore. Judah was soaring. Flying to the moon. The woman of his dreams loved him! If he wasn't worried about looking like a dork he would do a jig right here and now.

Thank you, Lord, for answering my most fervent prayer.

"I lo—" he began to say before she cut him off.

"No, don't say it, Judah! You need to know something first. Something important." Her voice sounded sharp and filled with urgency. Considering the circumstances, it felt off somehow.

"Nothing's more important than telling you how I feel." He leaned in and placed a searing kiss on her lips. Autumn broke off the kiss and took a step away from him. She bowed her head so he couldn't look into her eyes. At the moment Judah was flying blind. He had no idea what was going on with Autumn. He was caught up in all these conflicting signals she was sending out. She loved him but her expression looked like she was all doom and gloom.

Judah reached out and tilted her chin up. "Hey. What is it? Talk to me."

Her lips were trembling. "I lied to you twelve years ago, Judah."

Judah swallowed hard. He didn't say anything. Autumn needed to explain what she was talking about. Suddenly it seemed as if all the air had left his lungs. His entire body froze. Here it was. The thing that would get in the way of their happiness. By this time, he was sitting up straight on the couch. Not a single muscle in his body was relaxed.

"When I broke up with you it wasn't because I didn't love you. It was because I did." Her body shuddered. "A doctor told me I wouldn't be able to bear any children. That rocked me to my core. It felt as if our entire future was in ruins. I knew you wanted kids more than anything."

"No," he said hoarsely, "I wanted *you* more than anything."

"I kept thinking about all of our conversations about the future and how they revolved around having kids together. It was so hard to imagine you giving up that dream for me."

"But I would have," Judah responded. "Without question."

She bit her lip. "I didn't think you should have had to make that sacrifice."

Judah was hearing the words coming out of Autumn's mouth, but he wasn't understanding any of it. Infertility? A medical issue. She hadn't told him a single thing about this diagnosis at the time. Why would she have withheld that information from him?

"But you're pregnant now. You're not infertile," he said woodenly. This didn't seem real. She couldn't have done this ridiculous thing. Autumn wasn't capable of such a deception. Or of making such a random decision that had affected them both.

"I had surgery for my medical condition a few years ago," she continued. "Endometriosis. When the polyps were removed it allowed me to conceive. I wasn't given that option back then. It made a world of difference for me."

Judah lowered his head into his hands. If he'd been standing his legs might have buckled underneath him. All this time he had been waiting for the other shoe to drop and now it had. This, he thought, was why he'd never completely trusted Autumn. He'd known deep down that she was going to hurt him. And here it was. A bomb from the past that she had just detonated.

Everything had blown up in his face. What they'd been building had been torn apart in one moment.

"Judah, I know this is a lot to absorb, but I had to tell you."

He scoffed. "You *had* to tell me? Twelve years later?"

"Moving away from Alaska allowed me to stuff it down so I didn't have to think about it. I've always regretted it. You have no idea how much I've wished I'd taken another route." Tears ran down her face, but he tried his hardest not to be moved by her emotion. He was the one who had been lied to for all this time. She wasn't going to make herself the victim!

"But you didn't. You broke my heart." He stood up, fueled by the need to keep some physical distance between them. It felt painful to even look at Autumn.

"Other than having this baby," Autumn said, pressing her hands against her belly, "you're the one dream I've held in my heart. I knew if we had any hopes of a future together—and I so hope we do—that I needed to be honest with you. It's been a long time coming, but my heart has always been in the right place."

At this point he had heard enough. Nothing coming from Autumn's lips was resonating with him. It was all just white noise. His own heart ached too much for him to bear. This was soul crushing.

"I've got to get out of here." He spit the words out of his mouth.

Judah staggered out of the room and headed down the

hall. He reached for his jacket on the peg and jammed his arms through the sleeves. He quickly followed suit with his boots, stuffing his feet inside with jerky movements.

"Please, Judah. Don't go. Not like this," Autumn pleaded. "I know you're furious with me, but I'm here to talk this through. However long it takes."

He turned back toward her. "I'm not angry. Frankly, I'm too stunned to feel anything other than shock and disappointment. You basically changed the course of my life and never gave me any say in the matter. You decided my future. *Our* future." He let out a brittle laugh. "And you clearly didn't trust me enough to know I would have stuck by your side come what may. Because that would have been my choice. To love you wholly and unconditionally. I could have dealt with your diagnosis with grace and we could have explored other options. Face it, Autumn. You didn't believe in me or us. Moving forward, how in the world could I ever feel secure that you wouldn't bail on me again?"

Judah heard Autumn let out a sob as he wrenched the front door open and headed out into the Alaskan night. Snow was falling at a fast clip and he could barely make his way toward his truck between the moisture in his eyes and the fluffy white stuff. His breathing was heavier than normal. Everything had slipped away from him in an instant. After so much suffering in his past, he'd truly believed that he was headed toward happiness. But his joy had been fleeting.

Autumn wasn't the woman he'd believed her to be. She was nothing more than a figment of his imagination.

* * *

Autumn watched from the front window as Judah drove away from her. Maybe for the last time. She couldn't imagine anyone forgiving something so grievous. As his taillights blazed red against the falling snow, Autumn pressed her hand against her mouth to stop herself from crying out again. She didn't want to get too upset due to the baby, even though it felt as if her world was crashing and burning all around her. From all the reading she had done about having a baby, Autumn had learned that babies could absorb their mother's emotions. She needed to take deep breaths.

Judah had been completely knocked off-kilter by her confession. At some point it seemed as if he had just shut down. It had all been too much for him to carry on his shoulders.

He hadn't yelled or raged at her.

He hadn't even raised his voice.

Maybe it would have been better if he had. Anger faded over time, but shock and disgust lingered. She had never felt more ashamed of herself in her life. Viewing the situation through Judah's eyes had been devastating. Although she wished that it was possible to go back in time and fix things, life didn't work that way. All she could do was try and make amends with Judah.

But how? What could she possibly do to repair the damage she'd caused? She didn't truly believe any more words could be spoken. She'd done her best to explain her rationale for having gone down that destructive path in the first place. She had been dealing with so many emotions that she hadn't been able to handle. Fear. Sorrow.

Shock over her infertility diagnosis. And above all, an unwillingness for Judah to have to sacrifice his dreams for her. Of course she now knew her actions had been misguided, but it was too late to turn back the tide. Judah was right. There had been a domino effect as the result of her lie. In the end, there was nothing she could say to him that would justify her actions.

For now, she could pray and find comfort in Him. No matter what she'd done, He would never forsake her. Autumn knelt down on the floor. She crossed her hands in prayerlike fashion and closed her eyes.

God, please show me the way. Let me be a salve for Judah's pain. Even if he can't forgive me, allow me to help him as he continues his journey toward healing.

The snow was coming down now fast and furiously as Judah headed home. The storm had started hours earlier than expected. He could barely see five feet ahead of him on the road. Visibility was poor and his truck was skidding all over the place. He pulled the truck over to the side of the road, knowing his emotions combined with the hazardous conditions were a bad combination. In a perfect world he wouldn't be driving right now.

He idled his truck and looked outside his window, trying to monitor the situation as best he could. The ache inside him wasn't fiery or explosive. He felt completely depleted. All he'd wanted was to spend a simple night with the woman he loved. Watching movies. Eating popcorn. Instead he had been taken on a wild roller-coaster ride that made him question everything.

It hurt so badly to know she hadn't trusted him. What had he ever done to make her doubt him?

Judah laid his head on the steering wheel and let out an agonized sigh. Autumn had come back into his life and brought him so much joy. Because of her, Judah had found his way back to his faith.

What if something happened to Autumn? The thought crashed over him like a powerful wave. He had learned through losing Mary and Zane that one never knew when someone might be taken in an instant. He had left her without saying goodbye. Judah hadn't wanted to look in her eyes. Maybe a part of him had known he would have headed straight back into her arms if he did so.

A moment of clarity struck him. Judah had loved this woman for most of his life. This was their second chance to get things right. He knew the universe rarely handed out do-overs. And he'd lost so much in his life already that could never be replaced. Despite the fact that he felt stunned by her admission, Judah knew he wanted to walk through the rest of his days with Autumn by his side. She made him a better man. When she was with him Judah felt hopeful. She had given him way more than she'd taken.

He knew with a deep certainty that everything she'd done had been born out of love for him. Misguided. Foolish. Shortsighted. But genuinely from the heart.

He needed to see Autumn, to talk things through with her. And he didn't want to wait until morning to see her beautiful face. Tomorrow wasn't a given for anyone. The distance between his location and Cecily's house was less than if he headed home. And this storm wasn't letting up anytime soon. Judah carefully got off the shoulder of the road and turned his truck around so that he was now traveling in the direction he'd just come from.

What should have been a twenty-minute ride took nearly an hour as Judah white-knuckled his way down the slippery, snow-packed road. The entire way he was praying for safe travels. When he finally pulled up in front of the house, Judah was happy to see a few lights were still blazing inside. With his heart in his throat, Judah trudged up to the front door and banged on it a few times in rapid succession. He was impatient to see Autumn. Eager to take her in his arms and put this whole matter to rest.

When the door swung open, Autumn was standing there with a stunned look stamped on her face. "Judah! You're back. Come on inside."

Covered in snow and chilled to the bone, Judah walked into the house. The cozy warmth enveloped him, making him wish he'd never left in the first place.

"Did something happen with the storm?" Autumn asked as she began helping him take his parka off. "Sit down," she instructed. "Let me help with your boots."

Judah sank down on to a wooden chair as Autumn tugged at his boots until they came off.

"So what happened?" Autumn asked, looking up at him. "It's bad out there."

Judah rubbed his hands together. "It got so nasty that I had to pull off the road."

"Oh no. That's terrible," Autumn said, letting out a fretful sound.

"Actually it wasn't as bad as it sounds. Being there gave me time to think. I don't want to squander our second chance. I don't intend to lose you a second time. I love you, Autumn. I never imagined I would love anyone again after losing Mary. But then you came crashing back into my life, reminding me at every turn that I have a lot of living ahead of me."

"Judah. Are you saying that you forgive me?" Autumn asked. Her voice trembled.

He pulled her down so she was perched on his lap. "Of course I forgive you. You're human. And I know you must've been struggling with the news you received. But now you're owning it." He winked at her. "It took you twelve years to get around to it, but you did it."

Autumn covered her face and let out a groan. "Don't remind me," she wailed.

"I'm sorry. Bad joke. It struck me when I was in the truck that you didn't have to tell me a thing. I would have never known. You could have shoved it all under the rug."

She shook her head. "No, I couldn't do that. It would have tainted our future, Judah. I couldn't take that risk."

He reached up and grazed her cheek with his thumb. "That's why I love you so much. You never take the easy path in whatever you do, whether it's writing an ambitious article or facing your past mistakes. Or starting over in your hometown."

"As a pregnant lady no less," she said, pointing to her belly.

"A brave pregnant lady," Judah said, squeezing her hand.

"I've been thinking a lot about what I did," Autumn

said. "I'm just now realizing that I wasn't as sure of us as I thought I was. If I had been secure I would have trusted you to stand by my side through my infertility diagnosis. I would have known that I was enough, just me. Somehow I thought you needed me as a package deal along with babies."

"How could you ever think that, Autumn?" He reached out and grazed the side of her face with his palm. "I loved you wholeheartedly. Completely. If it had been up to me, we would have walked through life together. I loved Mary, but you were the great love of my life. My other half. I would have chosen you time and again."

She blinked away tears. "Oh, Judah. I loved you then and I love you now. I'm so grateful for your grace in forgiving me."

"My motives are a bit selfish. I want to be with you, Autumn, for the long haul. I don't want there to be anything standing between us," Judah said. "Not the past. Not things left unspoken. Nothing."

"I know that I can trust you, Judah, with anything. It's something I should have known back then, but I didn't."

"It's okay. From now on we're just going to think of it as something that happened on our journey. We can't dwell on it."

"I'm so happy I came back home to Serenity Peak." She placed her arms around his neck and pressed a kiss against his cheek.

"I'm so happy you're mine," Judah said, leaning in for another sweet kiss. Autumn happily obliged.

Happiness was theirs for the taking. There were no

obstacles standing in their way now. A glorious future stretched out before them. With faith, hope and an abundance of love, Autumn and Judah would make their second chance love story last a lifetime.

Epilogue

The sun was shining brilliantly on a warm September day in Serenity Peak. Autumn and Judah had driven out to the hot springs for an end of summer picnic and to celebrate the birth of the baby boy she'd decided to name River. Judah had agreed that it was a strong and powerful name. Over the past few months, all of the most important things had come into sharp focus for them. Love. Forgiveness. Hope. New beginnings.

Both her and Judah's families were soundly in their corner as their relationship continued to blossom. For Autumn it demonstrated the strong ties that bound families together. She would never stop treasuring her beautiful family. Or Judah.

Autumn shook her head. "Sometimes it feels like none of this can be real. How did all of my dreams come true at the same time?"

"Because you're worthy of every happiness this world has to offer." He leaned over and kissed her. "And I'm going to make sure the blessings keep coming."

"My editor told me this morning that my articles are some of the most read on the *Tribune*'s website," Autumn said. She was bursting with pride over how well her work was being received by the public. Her piece on the hardworking fishermen in Alaska was a nice contrast to her hard hitting article about fraud in the industry. Once fraud charges had been levied against two fishing operations in the Kenai Peninsula, Autumn had been able to conclude the series with a bang. It gave her confidence to continue to write the stories of her heart and to dig deep to unearth the truth when necessary.

Thankfully, the rumors about Judah had fizzled out once arrests had been made. He no longer felt as if he was the subject of whispers and finger pointing.

"I'm proud of you, Autumn. I know it wasn't easy packing up your whole life and coming back to Serenity Peak. But you followed your heart and it led you straight back to me."

"You've made me very happy, Judah. I came back home for the sake of this little guy," she said, touching River's little toes as he slept, "but you were the icing on the cake. An unexpected blessing."

"Ditto. I thought that I was going to be walking through life alone until you opened my heart up again. You dared me to start living again."

"You did all the heavy lifting." She reached out and caressed his cheek. "The courage you've shown in moving forward is awe-inspiring." Moisture pooled in her eyes. "You could have walled yourself up for the rest of your days. But you chose to live again…and love. I'm so blessed to be the recipient of this big old heart."

She placed her palm on his chest, right over his thumping heart.

He entwined her hand with his own. "Truth is, you've always owned a large chunk of my heart. Life took us both in other directions. God gave me Mary and Zane. He blessed you with River. And now He is making a way for us. That's pretty spectacular."

She squeezed his hand. "God is good, my love. And so are you. You're a very special man. I'm glad you're my person."

"Right back at you." He leaned over and placed a kiss on her lips. "I'm not sure any of this would have happened without you. And River. You showed me that I was still a man of faith and that I deserved to be part of the living. That knowledge transformed me."

"You didn't ever lose your faith, Judah. You simply got sidetracked. By loss and grief. By the storms of life that crashed over you. I'm so sorry you had to endure all of that pain."

"It brought me to my knees, but something inside of me never gave up. Even when I wanted to hide away from the world and wallow, I still got a thrill out of fishing and visiting Ida…and you. When I first saw you stranded in the rainstorm it was as if my entire body was jolted back to life."

"You came to my rescue that day and every day since then, Judah Campbell."

"We rescued each other, sweetheart. If not for you I would still be stuck in the past and licking my wounds. You brought me back into the world. And for that I'll always be grateful."

For a few moments they sat in companionable silence as they enjoyed the balmy weather and the beauty of their lovingly created family.

"I have something to ask you," Autumn said, looking deeply into Judah's eyes.

Judah let out a groan. "Uh-oh. The last time you said those words to me you were on assignment and wanted my help. What is it this time?" He made a face, which earned him a slight push from Autumn.

"Be nice. This is serious business," Autumn said in a solemn tone.

Judah's expression turned on a dime into a somber one. "Okay, I'm listening," he said.

She reached out and linked their hands. "I, Autumn Hines, want to humbly ask you to do me the honor of becoming my husband." She reached out and placed a finger on his lips. "Shh. Before you say a word, there are a few things I'd like to tell you. We loved and we lost one another. We've loved other people between then and now. But I've always held on to a piece of you, Judah. I buried it so deeply inside of me that I didn't even realize it myself until I came back home. Having you in my life…and River's is a dream come true. I'm happier than I've ever been and that's because of you, my sweet Judah. That was all part of the journey that led us to each other."

"Autumn, the answer is yes," Judah said in an exuberant voice. "It seems as if I've waited a lifetime for this moment. I've lived enough life to know that we have to seize happiness when it's within reach." He cupped her face in his hands. "I can't wait to start our journey and grow old together. I want to walk through this life with you, sweetheart."

Autumn leaned in and placed her arms around Judah's neck. "And maybe we can give River a sibling... or two."

Judah threw back his head in laughter. "If God blesses us with more kids that will be amazing. The more the merrier," Judah said. "But if it's only just the three of us, I'll be the happiest man in Alaska."

Autumn turned her face up toward Judah. "And I'll be the happiest woman because of what you've brought to my life." He kissed her then—tenderly, lovingly—whispering, "Forever" as his lips brushed against hers.

Peace. Love. Forgiveness. They had found their blissful happily ever after right here in Serenity Peak. For now and for always, they would be at each other's side.

* * * * *

If you enjoyed this story, look for these other books by Belle Calhoune:

Hiding in Alaska
Their Alaskan Past
An Alaskan Christmas Promise

Dear Reader

Welcome to Serenity Peak, Alaska. There's something so thrilling about introducing a new town to readers. There are so many possibilities to explore and stories to be told. It's all a fresh slate. I've left a few breadcrumbs in this book about possible future lead characters who'll have their own love stories.

I hope you enjoyed Autumn and Judah's love story. Judah is a man who has lost his entire world through a terrible accident. Steeped in grief and bitterness, it's hard for him to find a path forward. Autumn returns to Serenity Peak in the hopes of creating a new life for herself and the baby she's carrying. As a single mother she's facing challenges that might make her journey all the more difficult. When the two reunite there is a connection that they both feel even though they resist the attraction.

There are a few themes—forgiveness, resilience, grace—that run through this book. I enjoyed writing Autumn and Judah—two flawed characters who deserve a shot at happily ever after.

As always I'm thrilled to be a part of the Harlequin Love Inspired author team. I love writing inspirational romance and crafting happily ever afters. You can find me on my Author Belle Calhoune Facebook page and join my newsletter on bellecalhoune.com.

Blessings,
Belle

COMING NEXT MONTH FROM
Love Inspired

THEIR AMISH SECRET
Amish Country Matches • by Patricia Johns

Putting the past behind her is all single Amish mother Claire Glick wants. But when old love Joel Beiler shows up on her doorstep in the middle of a harrowing storm, it could jeopardize everything she's worked for—including her best-kept secret...

THE QUILTER'S SCANDALOUS PAST
by Patrice Lewis

Esther Yoder's family must sell their mercantile store, and when an out-of-town buyer expresses interest, Esther is thrilled. Then she learns the buyer is Joseph Kemp—the man responsible for ruining her reputation. Can she set aside her feelings for the sake of the deal?

THE RANCHER'S SANCTUARY
K-9 Companions • by Linda Goodnight

With zero ranching experience, greenhorn Nathan Garrison has six months to reopen an abandoned guest ranch—or lose it forever. So he hires scarred cowgirl Monroe Matheson to show him the ropes. As they work together, will secrets from the past ruin their chance at love?

THE BABY INHERITANCE
Lazy M Ranch • by Tina Radcliffe

Life changes forever when rancher Drew Morgan inherits his best friend's baby. But when he learns professor Sadie Ross is also part of the deal, things get complicated. Neither one of them is ready for domestic bliss, but sweet baby Mae might change their minds...

MOTHER FOR A MONTH
by Zoey Marie Jackson

Career-weary Sienna King yearns to become a mother, and opportunity knocks when know-it-all reporter Joel Armstrong comes to her with an unusual proposal. Putting aside their differences, they must work together to care for his infant nephew, but what happens when their pretend family starts to feel real?

THE NANNY NEXT DOOR
Second Chance Blessings • by Jenna Mindel

Grieving widower Jackson Taylor moves to small-town Michigan for the sake of his girls. When he hires his attractive next-door neighbor, Maddie Williams, to be their nanny, it could be more than he bargained for as the line between personal and professional starts to blur...

LOOK FOR THESE AND OTHER LOVE INSPIRED BOOKS WHEREVER BOOKS ARE SOLD, INCLUDING MOST BOOKSTORES, SUPERMARKETS, DISCOUNT STORES AND DRUGSTORES.

LICNM0323

HARLEQUIN PLUS

Try the best multimedia subscription service for romance readers like you!

Read, Watch and Play.

Experience the easiest way to get the romance content you crave.

Start your **FREE TRIAL** at
<u>www.harlequinplus.com/freetrial</u>.